UNTOUCHABLE

Eric Brown lives in Haworth, Yorkshire and is a
full-time writer. He has written four science
fiction and over forty short stories, which have
received much critical acclaim. This is his first
novel for Orion.

D0259641

Other titles in
THE WEB series

GULLIVERZONE

DREAMCASTLE

SPIDERBITE

LIGHTSTORM

SORCERESS

SERIES EDITOR
Simon Spanton

For more information about the books,
competitions and activities, check out our website:
http://www.orionbooks.co.uk.web

THE WEB

UNTOUCHABLE

◆

ERIC BROWN

Orion Children's Books
and

Dolphin Paperbacks

To Bob and Shirley Waugh,
and to the memory of Philip

First published in Great Britain in 1997
as an Orion hardback
and a Dolphin paperback
by Orion Children's Books
a division of Orion Publishing Group Ltd
Orion House
5 Upper St Martin's Lane
London WC2H 9EA

Copyright © Eric Brown 1997

The right of Eric Brown to be identified as the author
of this work has been asserted.

All rights reserved. No part of this publication may be
reproduced, stored in a retrieval system, or transmitted,
in any form or by any means, electronic, mechanical,
photocopying, recording or otherwise, without the prior
permission of Orion Children's Books.

A catalogue record for this book is available
from the British Library

Typeset at The Spartan Press Ltd,
Lymington, Hants
Printed and bound by Clays Ltd, St Ives plc

ISBN 1 85881 528 2 (hb)
ISBN 1 85881 426 X (pb)

627622
MORAY COUNCIL
Department of Technical
& Leisure Services
JCY

CONTENTS

CHAPTER ONE

ANA AND AJAY

That June, the monsoon rains came early to New Delhi.

Ana Devi crouched on the pavement outside the Union Coffee House, listening to the downpour drumming on the awning overhead. Above the city, the night sky was patched with a dozen hologram advertisements. A thousand auto-rickshaws and mopeds buzzed like angry wasps around the roundabout of Connaught Place.

Ajay slept beside her, his head resting on her shoulder. It was still early in the evening but her brother was only six years old and needed his sleep.

With his eyes closed, lips smiling at something in his dreams, Ajay looked perfect. Ana touched his cheek with her fingertips.

She stared out into the night, alert for danger, or the arrival of a car full of rich people.

The holo-ads marched across the night sky: 3-D images of perfect kitchens, men and women in fabulous clothes, exotic holiday resorts . . . Ana had once heard someone say that these images were the cinema of the people, but she thought they were more like glimpses of heaven.

She often spent hours gazing up at the light show, dreaming of being able to afford the luxuries glittering far above her. She wondered what it must be like to open a cooler and take out enough food to fill your stomach.

Now and again, giant words flashed across the sky in Hindi and English. Over the years Ana had taught herself to read both languages. INDIA IS GREAT IN THE TWENTY-FIRST CENTURY! she read, and, VOTE NATIONAL HARIJAN PARTY FOR A CHANGE!

She could read the words but often they made no sense.

She turned her attention to the cars speeding by on the road. She could easily spend hours staring up at the holograms but she had to watch out for Deepak Rao.

The thought of him made her skin crawl with fear.

A car pulled up in front of the restaurant. Ana stared with wide eyes, her heart beating fast. The car was slim and sleek, as silver as a new rupee coin.

As gently as she could, she leaned Ajay's head back against the restaurant window and struggled upright. She found her wooden crutch and pushed herself towards the car, the stump of her right leg hanging useless beneath her shorts.

The car doors lifted like the wings of an insect. Four people climbed out, tall men and women dressed in dark suits and colourful saris. Ana noticed the wink of gold and jewellery, caught the scent of expensive perfumes.

They moved from the car, chatting and laughing amongst themselves. They worked at not noticing her. Ana pushed herself before them, hand outstretched. 'Baksheesh, sir. Just one rupee,' she pleaded in Hindi.

A bearded man waved a lazy hand. '*Chalo*, girl. Go away!'

'You give me rupee, I go away, ah-cha, sir? See, I speak English. Ana not uneducated girl.'

The man gazed down and moved around her as if she were an infected dog.

She hobbled over to a woman dressed in a crimson and gold sari and pressed her palms together beneath her chin. 'Namaste, memsahib,' she whispered. 'One rupee for food?'

The woman stared at Ana, her expression sour. Ana had

seen the same look on the faces of many Brahmin women. They regarded her as less than an insect, a pest to be ignored or swept aside.

The woman spat. '*Chalo*, gutter rat! Away!' She hurried past Ana, joined her friends and entered the restaurant. As the door opened, the odour of tandoori chapatis and spiced masala wafted out, reminding Ana of her empty belly.

One of the high-caste men was talking to the doorman in the entrance. As Ana watched, he handed the doorman a note and glanced across at her.

A note! Then he was giving the doorman at least ten rupees!

The doorman crossed the pavement to where Ana was standing. 'Your lucky day, monkey. Rich businessmen. Brahmins.' He waved the note. 'Ten rupees.'

Ana stared at him. 'Fifty-fifty, ah-cha?'

The doorman laughed. 'Five rupees for little monkey? Think again, girl!' He reached into the pocket of his long coat, pulled out some coins. He counted them into Ana's outstretched palm. 'One, two . . .' He stopped, making to pocket the rest of the coins. 'But I'm feeling generous today, monkey. Here's another. Three, ah-cha? Now go, *chalo*!'

Ana swung herself back to her station beneath the window. She wished that the businessman had given the ten rupees straight to her instead of to the doorman. But Brahmins were like that. They did not like dealing directly with her, kept contact to a minimum.

She was untouchable, after all.

She supposed that she should be grateful that the doorman was a good man. Many others would have kept all the rupees and kicked her into the gutter.

Ajay was awake.

He stared in Ana's direction, but slightly to the left. With his eyes open, his face was not so perfect. Where his big brown eyes should have been, white circles like the skin on sour milk regarded her blindly.

'Rupees, Ana?'

She sat down beside him, slipped an arm around his shoulders and smiled. 'Three rupees, Ajay. Tomorrow morning we'll go to Begum's stall and buy chaat and puri, ah-cha?'

His smile was wonderful to see, and Ana could almost ignore his staring, sightless eyes.

She slipped one rupee coin into the pocket of her shorts. The other two she pushed into the pouch she kept on a cord around her neck, under her vest.

Over the past two weeks she had managed to save more than fifty rupees. If she worked harder, kept awake for longer, she was sure she could save even more. Soon . . . well, maybe in a year or two, she would have saved enough rupees so that she could buy what she had dreamed about for years.

She remembered seeing the holo-programme a long time ago, when she had been seven and Ajay just two.

She had stared at it with wonder, hardly daring to believe what she was seeing and hearing. There were doctors and nurses in India who could give blind people new eyes – they could take away the old, imperfect eyes and replace them with big brown eyes that worked.

From that day, Ana had lived in hope.

For two eyes, the doctors at the miraculous hospital charged two thousand rupees . . .

Until two weeks ago, Ana and Ajay worked for Deepak Rao in the slums of Old Delhi. Rao gave his boys and girls a stinking room to sleep in, and every day took them in his beat-up van to different areas of the city where they would beg all day. Late at night he would return and pick them up. Back at the room he would take all their earnings and search them for any rupees they might have hidden. Then he would give each boy and girl one rupee for food.

Every day Ana and Ajay begged, and every day they earned just one rupee which they had to spend to keep themselves alive.

Ana had saved no money, so how could she buy Ajay new eyes?

Then, two weeks ago, when Deepak had beaten Ajay for not begging enough rupees in one day, Ana knew what she had to do.

The following day, when Deepak had dropped them off, she took Ajay's hand and marched him from the slums of Old Delhi, past the monorail station and down Chelmsford Road to Connaught Place. There she moved from restaurant to restaurant, never the same one twice, and begged baksheesh from the rich customers.

Now, hope was blooming like a flower within her chest – but at the same time she felt fear, too. Deepak Rao would not sit idly on his massive bottom and let her escape so easily. He would have spies looking for her and Ajay, and if he found them— The thought was enough to make her sick.

Many children had disappeared from Deepak's gang over the years. Deepak would gather the children together, comment on the fact of the missing boys and girls, and say: 'They tried to escape, like beasts of the field returning to the wild. So what do you do with stubborn animals?' And he would draw his forefinger across his throat in a cruel and final gesture.

Now, Ana tried to banish the image from her mind.

In time, she told herself, she *would* save enough money to buy Ajay his new eyes . . .

Through the window of the restaurant Ana could see the big screen on the wall. The diners ate their expensive meals and looked up from time to time.

'What can you see, Ana?' Ajay asked.

She focussed on the images, rather than just seeing them as a series of floating patterns. 'It's . . . I think it's the Mars mission, Ajay.' The astronauts were tumbling around in their spaceship, turning head over heels like slow-motion circus performers. Objects drifted through the air: pens, notebooks, drink cartons.

Ana knew about the mission to Mars but she still found it hard to believe.

She stared at the images coming all the way through space. The astronauts were sucking food from see-through bags. The stuff looked like split pea dal. Ana felt her belly rumble.

She described the pictures to Ajay.

He frowned. 'Why are they going to Mars, Ana?' he asked.

'It's called,' she tried to recall the word she'd heard, '. . . *progress*.'

'What does that mean?'

They had sealed thirty men and women in three space ships and shot them off to Mars with enough food and water to last them for months, and they called it progress.

'I don't know what it means,' she said. 'Now go to sleep, Ajay, ah-cha?'

Ana was awoken by a loud shout.

She looked around, angry with herself for falling asleep. A kid stood across the road, pointing towards her and Ajay. He seemed too afraid to come any closer. 'There they are!' he yelled in Hindi.

Then Ana saw the van, and felt a sickening sensation in the pit of her stomach. Deepak Rao's battered green Nissan transporter came to a jerking halt a hundred metres away, then reversed along the road towards them. Ana saw Rao's big face hanging out of the window, glaring murderously at her through the teeming rain.

She screamed and pushed Ajay to his feet. 'Run!' she cried.

Ana held on to his shoulders and they ran. Her own leg acted as a third as they sprinted along the covered pavement in front of the lighted shopfronts. Over the years, in time of danger, they had often managed to escape like this. Ajay acting as her legs, while Ana was his eyes.

She heard shouts far behind her, the sound of a revving engine.

Many of the streets in the centre of New Delhi were curved, built in circular patterns by the British in the last century. This one curved away around Connaught Place Park with no break for side street or alley for a hundred metres. Ana considered crossing the road and entering the park – but then Rao would know where she was, and it would only be a matter of time before he found them. It would be better to try and escape down the side streets and alleys around Janpath.

At last they came to a corner. Ajay was panting at having to bear her weight. 'Turn left!' Ana called.

Without slowing, less fearful of what he might bump into than what was in pursuit, Ajay veered to the left. They raced down another wide street like the winning team in a three-legged race. Ana glanced over her shoulder and saw the green van turn the corner and accelerate after them.

She gave a terrified yelp. A metre ahead was the dark opening of a narrow alleyway. They dived into it and kept on running. At least now Rao would be unable to follow them in his van. He would have to give chase on foot. Deepak Rao was the size of an elephant. Ana had never seen him run. She began to think that this time they might get away.

The rain beat down, soaking them to the skin. She had stubbed her bare foot somewhere along the way, and every step was painful. Exhausted, Ajay was slowing down. She heard him sob with every breath, and tried to find the words to urge him on.

They ran through the darkness. The alley opened out and was crossed by a wider, lighted street. Cars and bicycles passed back and forth through the pounding monsoon downpour. Across the street, Ana saw another dark alley. If only they could get through the traffic and disappear into it— She looked over her shoulder. There was no sign of Rao or his helpers.

They emerged on to the busy street and stopped. Cars sped through the night in a continuous procession. Ana looked over her shoulder and saw a dark shape in the shadows of the alley behind her.

When she looked back at the road, there was a gap in the traffic. Sobbing in relief, she yelled at Ajay to run. They limped halfway across the road, stopped to let a battered coach pass, then ran the rest of the way and hurried down the alley. Behind them, the traffic had closed up again, halting Deepak Rao's pursuit.

She urged Ajay on, telling him that they were almost safe. 'Not far now. We're nearly there. But we've got to keep on, ah-cha? Then we'll stop and sleep.'

They turned left down a quiet street and slowed to a painful limp. They came to a road busy with cars and auto-rickshaws, turned left and slowed to a walk. A small voice in her head told Ana that they were not safe yet, that they should still be running. But she could run no further, and she knew that Ajay was exhausted too. They would walk a while, then head west before finding a concealed place to spend the night.

After that . . . perhaps they ought to leave the city

altogether, take a train south to Bombay or east to Calcutta. Deepak Rao would never find them then.

Later, she told herself that she should not have been thinking of the future. She should have concentrated on the present, on the danger they were still in. She might then have avoided what happened next.

She heard a deafening shout to her left. She looked down an alley and saw the small figure of a kid. She turned to run the other way, swinging Ajay with her, but not ten metres away stood Deepak Rao, breathing hard but grinning in triumph.

Ana cried out and dragged Ajay across the road, cars and mopeds flashing by in a blare of horns. Deepak Rao's shouts reached them like the wailing of a wronged spirit.

The cry frightened Ajay. He hesitated, unsure which way to turn, and Ana slipped and fell. Ajay ran into the middle of the road, turning this way and that in panic at losing her.

As Ana lay in the gutter, time seemed to stretch. In slow motion she watched a white Mercedes brake suddenly. Deepak Rao stepped from the pavement and grabbed Ajay's arm in a big fist winking with solid gold rings.

Ajay tried to struggle, but he was like an insect in the grip of a gorilla. Ana reached out, aware of the pain in her ribs, but her cry was lost in the roar of passing traffic. She ducked behind a parked car.

The door of the Mercedes swung open. Seated inside was the hunched figure of a woman. She was old, her face pale and terribly wrinkled – but what Ana noticed was that the woman was wearing a tight-fitting, silver dress cut short to reveal thin white legs. The woman stared out at Rao and Ajay, her lips moving with shouted orders.

Deepak Rao bundled Ajay into the back of the car beside the skeletal woman, and as the door swung shut, Ana caught a glimpse of a ring on the woman's hand. The Mercedes accelerated away into the rain-filled night.

Ana crawled along the gutter towards a taxi-rank, knowing that she had to give chase. She hauled herself upright and leaned panting against a taxi. She pulled open the door and fell inside.

She pointed to the Mercedes as it sped away. 'Follow . . . please follow!'

The driver gave her a withering look. 'You pay up front, I'll take you. Fifty rupees, girl.'

'Fifty?' she began. That was almost all her savings. But what was more important, her savings or Ajay? 'Ah-cha. Here. Now, quickly!'

She pulled fifty rupees from the pouch around her neck and thrust them at the driver.

Seconds later they were racing through the rain, buildings flashing by on either side. The taxi turned a corner, tipping Ana across the back seat. She righted herself and stared through the windscreen. She made out the tail-lights of the white Mercedes two hundred metres up ahead. It was heading south, into the rich district of the city.

Ana wondered what she would do when she found out where the Mercedes was taking Ajay. Why had Deepak Rao so readily handed him over to the old woman?

Five minutes later the taxi slowed.

'Hey! I said follow that car!'

'Like I said. You give me rupees, girl, and I'll follow.'

'But I *gave* you fifty!'

The driver laughed. 'Fifty got you this far. If you want to go any further, give me another fifty.'

Ana sobbed. 'But I've only got . . .' She tried to count her few remaining rupee coins. 'Please, you've got to help me—' But she should have known . . . When had anyone ever helped her for nothing?

The driver reached back between the seats, grabbed Ana's pouch and yanked. The cord snapped.

'Hey!' she began.

The taxi slowed. They were in a rich suburb of big houses and spacious gardens. The driver said, 'Get out.'

'No! You take me—'

He flipped a control switch and the back door opened. Ana felt a hand on her back as the driver pushed her from the car.

She hit the road with a painful smack and the taxi sped off into the night.

CHAPTER TWO

INTO THE WEB!

Ana pushed herself into a sitting position and looked around her. She was in the middle of a wet street with houses on either side, dark blocks against the brightly lit night sky. She was in the affluent suburbs south of central Delhi, where all the Brahmin businessmen and their families lived.

Her knee hurt, her forehead throbbed, and the palms of her hands smarted where they had scraped the ground. She was amazed that she had survived without breaking any bones.

Then she thought of Ajay and she felt a pain in her chest, as if a big fist had grabbed her heart and squeezed.

'Are you OK?'

The voice startled her. She looked around. A boy, older than her, was squatting on the pavement, staring. He had a round face and his dark hair was combed back and oiled. His clothes looked expensive.

'Do you speak English?' he asked.

Ana instantly disliked him. 'What does it matter to you?' she snapped.

Ana knew why he had asked. He had seen that she was a maimed beggar-girl, and he had wanted to show that he was superior by speaking English.

He was obviously surprised when she had replied in English as good as his.

'I saw what happened. Are you all right?'

She glared at him. 'What do you think? I was pushed from a car speeding at fifty miles an hour, and you ask if I'm all right—'

'More like five miles an hour, actually.'

'What?'

'I said, the car was only going at five miles an hour—'

Ana frowned and rubbed her knee. 'Well, it felt more like fifty . . .'

His eyes darted over her, taking in her soiled vest and shorts, the stump of her right leg. 'Do you make a habit of that?' he asked. 'Jumping out of moving cars?'

She glared at him. For a rich boy he was amazingly stupid. 'What do you think?'

He shrugged. 'What happened, then?'

She felt angry. How rude he was to ask such questions. 'Couldn't pay my fare,' she muttered. 'So he threw me out.'

'I'm sorry,' he said. 'Look, can I help you? Come back to the house – I'll give you something to eat and you can clean up.'

She was torn between accepting the offer of food and getting away from here.

'Well?' he asked.

'Just leave me alone!' she shouted. She looked around for her crutch.

But she'd left it back at the restaurant when she and Ajay had fled from Deepak.

It was this, the loss of her simple crutch which she had relied on for years, that finally made her cry.

She sat in the road, soaking wet and hurting, and wept.

The boy reached out, touched her shoulder. 'Please, let me—'

'Leave me alone!' She lashed out at him, dashing his hand away.

She struggled upright, hopped over to the fence and leaned against it, regaining her breath. The boy followed her.

She stumbled along the pavement, holding the fence for support.

'And how long will it take you to get home like that?' he asked.

'Just leave me alone! Please, please, leave me alone!'

'You're being stupid and stubborn. Why don't you let me help you?'

She stared at him. 'What do you want?' she asked. 'Why should you help me?'

He smiled. 'Because you *need* help. You've just fallen from a moving car. You can't walk. You look hungry and injured . . .'

She stopped, staring at him through her tears and strands of wet hair. 'Where do you live?' she asked.

The boy pointed to a big house. 'I have my own bungalow in the back garden,' he said. 'I'll get you some dry clothes and food.'

She considered his offer. She had never before met anyone willing to give her anything other than the odd rupee, and she was suspicious. 'Ah-cha. Just food and clothes – and then I go.'

'Suit yourself.' The boy shrugged. 'Here, lean on me.'

'Don't touch me! Get me a stick, something I can use as a crutch.'

The boy smiled to himself and shook his head. He disappeared into the garden. Ana leaned against the fence and stared at the mansions on either side of the street. This was another world, a place of luxury and privilege she had only ever seen in holo-ads.

The boy reappeared carrying a garden spade without its blade. The D-shaped handle fitted perfectly under her arm.

It was even a better crutch than her own. She hobbled along beside him as he walked into the grounds of the big house and up the drive. Half a dozen expensive cars were parked outside the house, and from an open window the sound of music and conversation drifted out.

The boy was speaking to her. 'I said, where do you live?'

She stared at him. How stupid and unthinking he was!

'My parents own a penthouse on Connaught Place,' she answered breezily. 'I have a few rooms overlooking the park.'

'No,' he said gently. 'I mean, seriously.'

'Where do you think I live? I sleep on the pavement outside the Union Coffee house with my— with—'

The thought of Ajay blocked her throat with emotion.

'With your family?'

'With my brother. I have no family.'

He nodded, led her past the house and into a back garden the size of a park. They approached a bungalow surrounded by trees. Ana stopped. 'I don't understand,' she said. 'All the other people like you . . . they want nothing to do with me. Rich people, Brahmins, they treat me like an animal—'

'My family is Brahmin,' he said. 'But I want nothing to do with that way of life. I've travelled, seen how other people live.'

She stared at him. 'You've been overseas?'

He smiled. 'And even farther,' he said mysteriously. He unlocked the door to his bungalow and stepped aside. 'Welcome to my world.'

Ana entered the lighted room, stopped and stared.

She had once read a story in a comic book about Aladdin's Cave, a place full of fabulous treasures, winking gold and glinting jewels. Now, she was reminded of Aladdin's Cave. There was no gold or jewels here, but there were other treasures. Her gaze raced around the room, stopping here and there before moving on to the next amazing object.

She stepped inside and moved around the room as if in a daze. She paused in front of something like a big television screen set into the wall. A multicoloured pattern was playing across its surface. Next to it was what she knew was a computer system, and next to that a musical instrument like an electric sitar. Chairs and sofas furnished the room, some even hanging from the ceiling on chains.

She turned in a circle, open-mouthed. She could have sold any one of these objects and bought food to last her months.

'Sit down and I'll get you a drier and a change of clothes.' He pointed to a chair and stepped through a door to a second room.

She sat in the chair, a black furry blob that looked more like some animal. She leaned back, and cried out as the chair moved beneath her. It flowed around her, taking hold of her waist as she sank into its spongy depths.

Ana kicked out and struggled, and at last escaped from its embrace. She sat on the floor, staring at the living chair.

The boy entered the room, carrying clothes.

'It attacked me!' Ana said. 'Your chair tried to attack me!'

'It's a foam-form,' he explained. 'It changes shape to suit the size of the person who sits on it.'

Ana felt herself blush.

He handed her the clothes, a white shirt, shorts and underwear, and a drier. She had never used an automated drier before, though she had seen them in the ads. It was a warm, egg-shaped object that you smoothed over your skin to magic away the moisture.

'I'll get you some food while you change,' the boy said.

While he was in the next room, Ana stripped off her wet clothes, dried herself, and pulled on the clean new shorts and shirt. The material was soft against her skin.

The boy returned with a tray full of samosas and two bulbs of milk. He placed it on the floor before Ana and sat crossed-legged opposite her.

He indicated that she should help herself, and Ana realized that it was almost a day since she had last eaten. She bit into a samosa, the spiced potato and peas the best things she had tasted in a long time.

She caught her reflection in the steel surface of some exercise machine across the room. She looked just like some rich schoolgirl in an ad. She felt a stab of guilt, and then pain that Ajay was not with her to share the experience. She decided that she would finish her meal and then return to Connaught Place. Then, she would try to find her brother.

The boy cleared his throat. 'I'm Sanjay, by the way.'

'Ana,' she said through a mouthful of samosa.

He indicated her leg. 'How did that happen, Ana?'

She stared at him, defiant. 'Are you always so rude with your friends?'

Sanjay smiled and shrugged. 'Where I spend much of my free time, we're open about everything.'

Ana took a long drink of milk, then wiped her lips with the back of her hand. 'If you must know, I was in a monorail accident,' she said.

Sanjay nodded. 'I'm sorry.'

Ana finished her milk and was about to thank him and leave when he said, 'Now, will you tell me what really happened?'

She glared at him. 'I told you – I was in a monorail accident.'

He laughed. 'No, I don't mean that – I mean, what happened earlier? Why were you thrown from the taxi?'

She stared at the crumbs caught in the folds of her new shorts. She suddenly wanted to tell this arrogant Brahmin boy about what had happened to her brother, to share her pain with him.

Perhaps, just perhaps, he might be able to help her find Ajay.

'Two weeks ago I ran away from Deepak Rao with my brother, Ajay,' she began. She told Sanjay how they had made their way to Connaught Place and kept hidden for two days, not daring to show their faces in case Rao should find them. Then, for a few hours each day, they had gone begging around the restaurants. The police had constantly moved them on, but rich people had given her and Ajay more rupees than they would normally earn in the slums of Old Delhi.

Then, Ana had become lax and fallen asleep, and Deepak Rao had found her. 'We ran and ran, but he chased us. I fell in the street and Ajay was picked up by an old woman in a white Mercedes.'

Sanjay was shaking his head. 'What could she want with your brother?'

Ana regarded her fingers. 'I don't know.'

'Can you describe her? Perhaps, if you gave her description to the police—'

Ana stared at him so hard that he stopped talking. For all his wealth, for all the education he must have had, he knew very little about the real world.

'The police!' she exclaimed. 'If I went to the police and told them that my brother had been taken, they'd laugh at me! Do you think they're bothered about the disappearance of a street kid?'

'I don't know . . . I thought—'

'Maybe if *you* had been taken, then they might do something.'

That silenced him. While he blushed and drank his milk, Ana looked around the room. She pointed at a reclining chair in the corner. 'Is that a Web-couch?'

Sanjay nodded. 'Do you know what the Web is?' he asked, surprised. He was doing it again, playing the arrogant little rich kid.

'Of course I do!' she said. Or, rather, she had a vague idea what the Web was.

Deepak Rao used the Web at the public VR-bar near the monorail station. He had bragged about its many wonders to the kids when he was drunk. 'I've been to a wonderful world!' he had shouted, swinging his bottle of whisky like a bell.

'Are you sure you know what it is?' Sanjay asked.

'It's like the movies, and you can step inside the film and take part in what's happening.'

'But you've never Webbed?'

She shook her head. 'But don't tell me – you have, right?'

He nodded, casual. 'Most days,' he said. 'Here, I'll show you.'

He stood and pulled the couch into the middle of the room. On the couch was what looked like the outline of a person – some kind of empty grey suit with wires attached, a control pad on its wrist, and a face mask.

'A Websuit and Web-couch. The latest Atari models,' he said smugly. 'You wear the suit, plug in, and use the wristpad to access the Web.'

Ana nodded, trying not to be too impressed.

Sanjay was looking at her, considering. 'Would you like to have a go?' he asked. 'Spin into the Web?'

'What, enjoy myself while Ajay is somewhere out there?' She grabbed her new crutch and struggled to stand up. 'No! I need to find my brother.'

'Ana, sit down, please. Think about it. What can you possibly do in the real world to get Ajay back?'

'At least I'll be looking for him! Which is more than I'd be doing if I went with you into the Web.'

Sanjay was shaking his head. 'You're wrong. I'll post MP reports on various Web sites.'

Ana stared at him, mystified. 'What do you mean?'

'I'll show you around the Web, and while I'm there I'll post missing person reports about your brother. Then, if Web users see Ajay in the real world they can contact me. Simple. So how about it?'

'I-I don't know. I've never done it before.'

'That doesn't matter. I'll show you the ropes.' He pointed across the room, to another Web-couch and Websuit. 'That's my spare suit for friends.' He glanced at her. 'You'll come?'

She wanted to ask him if she could have a bundle of rupees instead, but stopped herself. She gave a little nod. 'Ah-cha,' she said.

'Good.' He pulled the second couch and suit into the middle of the room next to the first. 'You can have my old suit. I'll use the Atari. Now, step into the suit.'

Ana hesitated, then picked up the suit. The material was cold, and clung to her skin. She found the opening in the back, sat on the edge of the couch and worked her good leg into the legging, then slipped the stump of her right leg into the second. The material hung loose where her right leg should have been. She pulled the suit around her body and worked her arms inside. It gripped her limbs, squeezing. Ana shivered.

She glanced at Sanjay. He stood in his own suit beside the couch, looking like a deep-sea diver. He slipped on his face mask and attached the control panel to his wrist. Ana did the same.

'Now, lie back on the couch and relax,' he told her. 'I'll plug us in.'

She lay back as instructed while Sanjay moved around the couches. She stared through her face mask at him, a part of her not believing that this was happening. Who would have thought, just one hour ago, that soon she would be entering the Web?

'I don't feel anything,' she said.

Sanjay lay down on his couch. 'Not yet, but you will,' he said. 'Just follow my instructions.'

He lifted his right wrist and pointed to the control pad. 'See the red button, Ana? That's the activator. Press it and you'll enter the Web. Once you're in the Web, you can press it at any time to get out. I'll show you all the other functions once we're in there, ah-cha?'

'Ah-cha,' Ana replied in a whisper.

'So . . . here goes,' Sanjay said. 'Into the Web!'

Ana reached out and pressed the red button—

Instantly her world was transformed.

CHAPTER THREE

TROPICANA BAY

'Where am I?' Ana screamed.

She was no longer in Sanjay's room. She was standing on a vast golden plain, a desert that seemed to extend forever beneath a bright blue sky. Before her was a series of multicoloured blocks like small houses.

'Relax, Ana,' Sanjay's voice said beside her. 'This is Level One, BB. We call those things building blocks.'

Ana turned. Sanjay – or rather someone like Sanjay – stood beside her. She gasped and stepped back. This Sanjay was much older and taller than the boy she knew. Although his face was still recognizably his own, it seemed more grown-up, and he was dressed in a smart white suit.

'I feel . . . funny,' Ana said.

Sanjay laughed. 'You'll get used to it, in time.'

'I don't know about that.'

Her brain knew that she was lying on her back – she could feel the tug of Realworld gravity as she lay on the Web-couch – and yet all her senses told her that she was standing upright. The contradictory sensations made her feel slightly ill.

Also . . .

Here she was in the Web, but she could smell the scents from the real world. She sniffed. She could smell the samosas she had just eaten, and the sweet incense that Sanjay burned in his room.

Sanjay saw her sniffing and laughed. 'You can't smell or taste things in the Web,' he said.

She glanced at him, at this changed, older Sanjay. The Web was truly a strange place.

'How did you do that?' she asked. 'How did you change yourself?'

Sanjay smiled down at her. 'Simple.' He indicated his wristpad. 'I programmed in how I wanted to look. I can make myself appear as anything. Watch.'

He tapped the keypad on his wrist.

He began to grow slowly taller, and taller, and at the same time thinner. His body became as thin as a drainpipe, his long arms hanging by his side like wires. His head grew. He bent double and leered down at her.

Ana backed off, whimpering.

'OK, OK,' Sanjay said in that superior way of his. His thin fingers touched the keypad again and he began to shrink. Within seconds he was the older version of Sanjay again.

Only then did Ana realize that she had taken two steps backwards.

Steps!

She had not taken actual *steps* for years.

She looked down at her body. She had *two* legs. She was wearing a white smock, and she had two perfect, brown legs.

'I-I don't understand,' she murmured. 'How is it possible? My leg—'

'The suit is relaying the sensations of your phantom limb to your brain,' Sanjay explained. But to Ana that was no explanation at all. 'Therefore, you *think* you have two legs. And in the Web that's all that matters.'

She stared down at her new leg. It *looked* just like her good leg, but at the same time it felt artificial. She moved her toes, and though she could see them, she had no feeling of movement.

She took a deep breath. For years she had been unable to run, really run, without the help of Ajay. Now . . .

She stepped forward, walking towards the coloured blocks. She had the sensation of really walking, her feet brushing the warm surface of Level One. She felt dizzy with delight.

Fearing that she might fall over, she increased her pace. She began running, thumping down on the ground with both feet, arms swinging. She knew that she was really lying down, yet all her senses told her that she was running. Her dizziness increased, made her head swim. She was moving with a slight limp, her new leg not as efficient as her good leg – but far, far better than the crutch she had used for so long in the real world.

Sanjay was beside her.

'And if you think that's special,' he said, 'just wait until you change your appearance.'

She shook her head. 'How do I do that?'

'Press the panel marked A on your pad,' Sanjay said.

She did so. A list appeared on a tiny screen beside the keypad: HEIGHT? COLOUR? AGE? DRESS STYLE?

'This is a simple program. It'll just alter your appearance as you are now. More sophisticated programs like mine will allow you to alter *everything*. How tall do you want to be?'

'I don't know . . .' She was small for her age. She had always dreamed of being taller. 'As tall as you are now?'

'OK, just tap in two metres.'

She followed his instructions. Instantly she seemed to grow. Her eye level shot up. Now she was as tall as Sanjay.

'Now, for colour and age just tap in what you desire. To stay the same just tap in S.'

Ana considered. She would stay the same colour, but make herself a little older.

Next to COLOUR? she tapped in S, and next to AGE? she tapped in 16.

'How do I change what I'm wearing?'

'Next to dress style tap in casual, or smart, or formal. The program has thousands of options, but it'll be quicker if you just stick to the simple ones.'

'Ah-cha . . .' She tapped in: smart. She had always wanted to be as well-dressed and sophisticated as the people in the holo-ads.

She looked down at her sixteen-year-old body. She was wearing a red knee-length dress and smart red shoes that felt odd on her feet.

'And now, Ana,' Sanjay said, 'are you ready to bat?'

She stared at him. 'What?'

'Blue-and-tone,' he said. 'Enter one of the worlds of the blocks. That one, for instance, is for the entertainment and recreation Web sites. How about a little E&R?'

He held out his arm, and she took it – amazed at the feel of the material of his white suit beneath her fingers. They strode towards the block, and the sensation of walking made her forget that in the real world she was lying on a Web-couch in Sanjay's bungalow.

They halted before the face of the block. 'Touch it,' Sanjay said.

Ana reached out, brushed the block with her fingertips. The red gloss rippled like the surface of a pond.

'Now, step through,' he said.

Holding tightly on to Sanjay's arm, Ana walked into the block. She heard a loud pinging in her ears and her vision was flooded briefly with a bright blue light.

And then, for the second time that day, her world was transformed.

Ana gasped.

It seemed that she was standing in the centre of a busy, bustling city. Buildings like skyscrapers reached high into the blue sky. Long, straight roads stretched between the buildings, and these avenues were thronged with a thousand different types of people and . . . *things*. She stared. Big spiders scurried around between humans of every size and shape. Some, she saw, had changed their appearances so that they had the heads of animals – gorillas, zebras and unicorns.

She turned her attention to the buildings and realized that they were not really buildings at all. On the surface of each construction was what looked like a vast cinema screen showing a different picture.

From time to time as she watched, a human or spider would walk *through* one of the screens and disappear.

'Welcome to E&R, Ana,' Sanjay said. 'There are thousands of blocks in this Webtown, and each block offers a different world of entertainment and recreation. We can enter whichever world we wish simply by stepping through the wall, or accessing the code through our keypads.'

Ana just stared, shaking her head in wonder. 'Where shall we go?'

'How about Tropicana Bay? It's very popular with New Delhi-ites.'

He led the way across to a skyscraper that showed a scene from paradise. A gently sloping beach stretched around the perfect circle of a bay, except that the water of the bay was more silver than blue, and the sand of the beach was red. Even the trees that fringed the foreshore were unlike any trees she had ever seen. Instead of green leaves they sported myriads of yellow flowers. Between the trees, groups of people sat around tables, chatting and laughing.

'Let's take a stroll around Tropicana Bay,' Sanjay suggested.

He took her hand, and Ana felt a sudden surge of wonder at what was happening to her. They stepped through the surface of the screen, Ana laughing aloud at the weird sensation of moving so easily from one world to another. She found herself walking towards the beach, the sunlight warm on her skin and a breeze blowing in her face.

Ana stopped and knelt by the silver sea. Sanjay watched her. 'Ana, what's wrong?'

She shook her head. She reached out and took a handful of water – except that it didn't feel like real water, but more like a million tiny diamonds.

Ana shook her head again, disbelieving.

'This is the first time,' she said, 'that I've ever seen the sea.'

Ana and Sanjay strolled along a promenade between the red sands of the beach and the grass of the foreshore. They passed other couples, well-dressed, sophisticated men and women like the people from the holo-ads. Ana found it hard to accept that she was a part of this incredible world.

She wondered what all these people were like in real life.

She remembered something. 'Hey, I thought you said you were going to post a missing person report?'

Sanjay tapped his wristpad. 'I've already posted the MP report, Ana – I've asked for any info about a six-year-old blind boy taken by Rao and a woman in a white Mercedes.'

'Ah-cha.'

They passed a kiosk that hired out jet-chutes. Reflected in the window, Ana caught sight of an attractive young woman in a red dress.

She stopped in her tracks and stared.

The young woman mimicked her movements, her gestures and facial expressions. Ana frowned, and so did the woman. She turned her head and the woman turned her head too. In the face staring out at her, Ana recognized herself, but more mature, even beautiful. She had breasts, and long legs, and her hair was long and sleek, not the tangled mess it was in real life.

She tried to feel the Websuit that she knew she was wearing, tried to detect the couch she was lying on, and only when she really concentrated could she feel the material of the suit that enveloped her and the sponginess of the couch beneath her.

Then she forgot that she was really in Sanjay's bungalow, and lost herself in the illusion.

'Sanjay!' someone called from the beach.

'Rom!' Sanjay raised a hand a waved.

A white boy with a shock of red hair came running across the sand. 'Hi there, Sanjay,' he said in an American accent. 'Who's the egg?'

'She's no egg, Rom. Meet Ana, a friend from India. Ana, this wise guy here is Rom, Web-wizard and all-round pain.'

Rom squinted from Ana to Sanjay. 'You trying to bite me? You sure she's not your kid sister? I can tell Ana's a first-timer.' He winked at her. 'How're you liking Webworld, Ana?'

She glared at him. 'I was having a great time until I met you.'

'Ow!' Rom yelped, shaking his hand as if stung. 'Hey, no hard feelings, OK? Friends?' He held out his hand.

She smiled. 'Friends,' she said, accepting his handshake.

Sanjay asked, 'Been anywhere venomous since last time?'

'You kidding? Have I told you about the Dreamcastle? It's a long story, Sanjay. Hairy!'

Ana looked from Sanjay to Rom, trying to work out what they were talking about.

'Hey,' Rom said, 'what're you doing now? How about a little jet-chuting?'

'Eight!' Sanjay said. 'You, Ana?'

Ana looked across the bay at the jet-chutes looping through the air. 'I think I'll just sit and watch you.'

'You sure? . . . Ah-cha.' He slapped Rom on the back. 'Let's do it!'

They hired a pair of jet-chutes and rose into the air. Ana watched them climb into the sky, waving and yelling like the kids they were as they circled high above the bay.

She strolled along the promenade, constantly amazed at the strange *reality* of this world. Here the surfaces were brighter than out there in the real world, more like the colours in a film. And surely things actually *moved* faster, too – or was this just her excited reaction to finding herself in the Web?

She was surprised at how friendly Rom had become, after his first few digs at her. In the real world he would never have looked twice at her, still less talked to her.

She found a café and thought about sitting down alongside all the other people. But something stopped her – how might all these well-dressed, beautiful people react if *she* sat down near them and ordered a drink?

In New Delhi, if she tried to enter an expensive café, begging for food, she would very quickly be chased out . . . and maybe even beaten.

But . . . she was not in New Delhi. She was no longer in the real world, she reminded herself.

She no longer looked like the twelve-year-old untouchable beggar girl that she really was.

She told herself – though it was very hard to believe – that she looked just as rich and good-looking and well-dressed as all these sophisticated people around her.

If she joined them, how would they know who she *really* was?

Even so, as she crossed the grass and sat down at an empty table, her heart was beating fast and she imagined that everyone was staring at her with distaste in their eyes.

A white-coated waiter approached her from an open-air bar. 'Can I get you something, Miss?'

Ana looked around, wondering who he might be talking to. But he was looking straight at her. Embarrassed, she opened her mouth to say something.

The waiter smiled. 'First-timer, yes? Then welcome to the Web. I can get you the house special, a daiquiri-synth slammer. Yes?'

Ana nodded. 'Yes, please.'

The waiter winked at her and hurried to the bar.

She sat in the sunlight and watched as he mixed her drink. She was aware of her heart hammering in her chest. It would take a lot of getting used to, being treated as an equal like this.

The waiter returned with her daiquiri-synth slammer, presented it to her with a bow and moved to the next table. Ana raised the long glass of sparkling blue liquid to her lips, wondering if it would be possible to drink in the Web.

She soon found out. The liquid did not enter her mouth, but seemed to fizz over her lips and across her face, blurring her vision and making her laugh at the tickling sensation. She noticed the other 'drinkers' around the bar lifting glasses to their lips, laughing . . .

She was about to take a second 'sip' when she saw a familiar figure seated at a table near the beach.

She almost dropped the glass, panic clutching at her chest.

It could not be true.

The man seated with the striking young blonde woman certainly looked like Deepak Rao, but he was much slimmer, and better dressed, and his face was younger than in reality. Ana recognized the shifty eyes, though, and the thick, revolting lips.

So this is where he came when he Webbed with the money earned by all his child-beggars.

Next to him, the blonde Western woman raised a glass to her lips. Ana recognized the tight-fitting silver dress, the thin face of the woman she'd seen in the white Mercedes.

Of course, the woman in the car had been old, hideously old – but here in the Web age counted for nothing.

This woman had taken her brother, and Ana had to find out what she had done with him. She wanted to confront Rao and the woman and demand to be told where Ajay was – but that would be stupid and dangerous.

She controlled her panicked breathing and considered the situation. She told herself that there was no chance of being recognized by Deepak Rao. He would not be expecting to see her here, and anyway she looked nothing like the beggar-girl she was in real life.

The table next to them was vacant. Ana knew that she should make her way across to it, try to listen in on what they were talking about.

She told herself she had nothing to fear. She stood up, her heart pounding.

Casually, she strolled through the grass to the empty table and sat down. Neither Deepak nor the woman had paid her the slightest attention.

She sipped her drink, straining to overhear their conversation.

'I need more . . .' the woman was saying.

'How many?' Rao replied. Ana would have recognized his voice anywhere. Even in the Web it was as sickly as ghee.

'How many can you get?'

'Oh . . .' Rao considered, stroking his moustache. 'Say . . . six more.'

'I want them by midday tomorrow, understood?'

'I understand perfectly. Do you require boys or girls?'

The woman waved. 'It makes no difference. Just so long as you bring me six children, you will get your money.'

Deepak Rao nodded with satisfaction and sipped his drink.

Ana wanted to scream at Rao and the woman, force them to tell her what they had done with her brother, but she knew that to show herself now would be a mistake. She had to be careful, very careful.

'You did say that one day you'd tell me where you were keeping them,' Rao said.

The woman gave him a superior look. 'I said "one day", Rao. Today is not the day.'

'Then tomorrow,' Rao smiled sickeningly. 'I would be intrigued to know what becomes of my children.'

'What makes you think I would trust you, Rao?'

Deepak Rao spread his hands in a humble gesture. 'But I have been your faithful servant now for . . . how many months? Have I not served your every need? Surely you can trust me by now?'

The woman gave him another contemptuous look, as if she were regarding a worm. 'We'll meet in the Web tomorrow morning at eight,' she said. 'If I feel in the mood, then I'll take you to the children. Meet me at these coordinates.' And she gave a series of letters and numbers that Ana had no hope of remembering.

'And now,' said the woman, 'time to scuttle. *Ciao*, Rao.'

As Ana watched, the woman touched the red button on her wristpad. What happened next made Ana stare in disbelief. The woman dissolved, became a swirling mass of coloured bubbles – just like the fizz in a glass of soft drink. Then the bubbles vanished and the woman was gone.

Deepak Rao sat alone, sipping his drink, a satisfied expression on his smug face.

Ana stood and hurried from the bar area, wanting to put as much distance as possible between Deepak Rao and herself.

She moved along the beach, looking into the sky for Sanjay.

'Hey, Ana! What's the rush?'

She turned. Sanjay was standing beside the kiosk, having returned his jet-chute. 'Ana, are you all right?'

'I've . . . I've just seen Deepak Rao and the woman who took Ajay! They were here!'

'Hey, calm down, Ana. Just calm down.'

'But I saw them. The woman said she wanted more children. Deepak's going to meet her in the Web tomorrow at eight, and she's going to show him where she keeps the kids!'

'Ana, slow down and start from the beginning. Tell me exactly what you heard.'

He sat her down at an empty table and Ana repeated what Deepak Rao and the woman had said.

Sanjay shook his head. 'I don't understand. Are you sure she keeps the kids in the Web?'

Ana nodded. 'That's what she said. She told Deepak Rao that maybe she'd take him to where she was keeping the children.'

'But you can't keep anyone in the Web! You can stay in here for a few hours, and then you start getting Web-sickness – the voms.'

'Sanjay, what is the woman doing to my brother and the other children?'

'I don't know, Ana.' He fell silent, then looked up. 'Does Deepak Rao use his own Websuit or does he go to a public VR-bar?' he asked.

'He uses the bar near the monorail station.'

'Good. We'll meet there just before eight in the morning.

If we BAT at the same time as Rao, then we'll be able to follow him. With luck and good disguise we'll be able to find out what's going on.'

Ana nodded. 'Ah-cha, Sanjay.'

'Hey, it's late, Ana. I need my sleep. I'm scuttling. See you back in Realworld.'

He pressed the red button on his wrist-pad, and seconds later Ana hit hers.

She found herself back in Sanjay's room, lying on the couch in the tight Websuit. She sat up, then stood and tried to take a step. She fell over, crying out in pain and bitter disappointment.

She sat up and stripped off the Websuit. She was Ana the beggar-girl again, Ana the untouchable, twelve years old with one leg and no money and a brother kidnapped by an evil old woman.

Ana stared about her. Everything seemed dull here in the real world. Sanjay was no longer the dashing young man he had been in the Web, and as he stripped off his suit he seemed to be moving in slow motion.

He smiled at her confusion. 'You'll get used to it, Ana. Things happen faster in the Web, so when you exit from it the real world seems slowed down.'

She nodded, looking for her crutch.

Sanjay said, 'If you like, you can spend the night here.'

Ana looked around the room. It was too comfortable, too luxurious. She was used to life on the streets.

'I'll see you in the morning near the VR-bar,' Ana said. She hesitated. 'How much will it cost to use the Web?'

Sanjay smiled. 'Nothing,' he said. 'I have a card that'll pay for us both.'

She found her new crutch and moved to the door. Sanjay followed her. 'Look, you can't walk all the way into New

Delhi. Take this and hire a taxi.' He forced a ten rupee note into her palm, and Ana did not object.

She left him with a small wave, limped from the grounds of the mansion and turned right, heading north. She came to a main road, and the taxi rank. She paused, thought about the luxury of taking a ride back to Connaught Place. She shook her head and limped on past the line of taxis.

She shoved the ten rupee note into the pocket of her shorts.

She had started saving for Ajay's eyes again.

CHAPTER FOUR

THE CHAMBER

Ana found it hard to believe that just one hour ago she had been in the Webworld of Tropicana Bay. She had strolled along the seashore, known what it was like to have two legs again. Now, her shoulder ached with the pressure of the crutch and her bare left foot was sore from the long walk.

Keeping to the quiet alleyways, she made her way to the city centre and the VR-bar. She would sleep in one of the doorways nearby, and then meet Sanjay outside the bar just before eight.

It was midnight and quiet along the darkened streets. Homeless families huddled in the doorways of every shop and those less fortunate slept out on the pavements. Rats scurried along the gutters, searching for scraps of food. Ana shivered, despite the warm wind. She thought of Sanjay and his comfortable bungalow.

Then she thought of Ajay. She had been with him for so long that she found it hard to believe that she was without him now. She half expected to turn and see him trotting along behind her, smiling at some private thought.

As she limped along the street, looking for an empty doorway, tears filled her eyes.

'Ana!' someone hissed from the shadow of a doorway. 'Ana Devi!'

She turned, her heart beating in panic.

A young boy appeared from the darkness, pushing himself along in a wheeled cart made from a flimsy fruit box.

'Prakesh!' Ana said.

She had known Prakesh for years. He worked for a friend of Deepak Rao's. Prakesh had no legs, and a voice like a songbird. He sang ragas outside the monorail station, earning many rupees for his master.

'Ana!' Prakesh hissed. 'You're in great danger.' He tugged her into the doorway.

She squatted down in the shadows beside him.

'Ana! Rao's looking for you. Rao and his kids – everyone! They're not sleeping tonight. They're searching every street in Delhi!'

'Do you know where they took Ajay?'

The boy made a pained face. 'Ajay was taken?' He shook his head. 'Sita, Nazreen, and Parveen have all disappeared, too, just like that – never seen again. Now Deepak wants you. He's angry, first that you ran away, then angry again that you got away tonight. He doesn't want the other children to think they can get away from him. He said "Whoever tells me where Ana Devi is, there's a reward of many rupees."'

He stared at her with big eyes. 'What're you going to do, Ana?'

She shrugged. 'Find somewhere to sleep tonight, somewhere safe.'

Prakesh reached out and gripped her wrist. 'Not here, Ana! Every fifteen minutes, Deepak drives along the street. Try the monorail station. Look, take my blanket, wrap yourself up so you can't be seen. Sleep at the station.'

Ana thanked him. 'Keep your blanket, Prakesh. I'll hide in an alley.'

'Ah-cha. Take care, Ana.'

She stood, fitted her crutch under her arm and moved

quickly from the doorway. As she hurried along she realized that she was the only moving figure in the quiet street. If Rao were to drive by now—

She tried to push the thought to the back of her mind. She had to hide until eight when she would meet Sanjay and follow Rao into the VR-bar, try to find out why he was selling children to the old woman.

It was past midnight now, and many of the hologram advertisements in the sky had closed down for the night, leaving great patches of darkness up above where the stars shone through. This meant that the streets were darker too and there were more shadows in which to hide from Deepak Rao.

Ana considered what Prakesh had told her, that Rao had offered a reward to anyone who found her. It meant that many people would be looking for her, eager for rupees. The thought made her angry and afraid.

She turned down a narrow sidestreet. During the day, this street was full of shops and stalls selling meat: lamb, chicken and goat. The street stank of blood and offal, and no one slept here at night. Maybe Deepak Rao would not think to come down here in search of her. She would find a doorway and doze until eight.

She stopped, her heart thumping like a drum. Ahead of her, at the end of the alley, she thought she saw a shadowy figure. She told herself that it could be anyone or anything, told herself that she should not be afraid. She squinted into the darkness. The figure was still there, tall and unmoving – staring at her.

Quickly, Ana swung herself around and set off back down the alley, a moan escaping from her lips. She stopped at a sound up ahead – a grumble of an old petrol engine.

In her fright, she almost stumbled and fell. She stared

down the alley. A green van – Deepak's old Nissan trans-porter – stood at the end of the alley, blocking her way.

She turned again. The tall dark figure was moving towards her. She was trapped – like a rat in a box. She wanted to scream at the unfairness of what was happening but knew that to show her anger and despair would be to show Deepak Rao how frightened she was – and she did not want to give him that satisfaction.

She hurried towards the van. He might capture her, but she would do her best to hit him with her crutch.

The door of the van opened, and at the same time a pair of hands gripped her from behind. She tried to struggle, but the man's hold was impossible to break.

Deepak Rao squeezed himself from the van like an overweight genie emerging from a battered lamp. He stood with his arms folded, looking down on Ana. 'You're a very stupid girl to think you could escape,' he said. 'You know that no one can get away from Deepak Rao.'

He nodded to the man holding her. 'Into the van,' he said.

The man gripped her with one huge arm, opened the back door of the transporter and tossed her inside. Ana fell heavily, managing to keep a tight hold on her crutch. The door slammed. Seconds later the engine started and the van trundled off.

She sat up, riding the painful bumps, and stared through the rear window at the passing streets. She hoped that at least she might soon be reunited with Ajay.

Five minutes later, the van slowed and stopped. She peered through the window. Her heart sank at the sight of the familiar interior of the warehouse where Rao had his base. She heard footsteps, and the doors were flung open. Deepak Rao stared in at her. 'Get out, girl!'

As the strong man Rajiv grabbed her ankle and dragged her out, she cracked her head on the back of the van. She cried aloud as she hit the floor. The strong man swept her up and carried her across the vast floor of the warehouse. Deepak Rao lifted a trapdoor and Rajiv set her down by the dark hole. He tried to pull her crutch from her grasp but Rao shook his head. 'Let her keep it.'

The strong man grunted, lifted Ana by one arm and lowered her into the hole.

Ana yelled in protest, feebly kicking her leg. The man dropped her and she hit the stone floor with a painful smack.

She had been here before, many years ago. This was the chamber where Deepak Rao kept his newly-found waifs and strays.

Four years ago, her uncle had been unable to feed and clothe Ana and Ajay any longer, and had turned them out on to the streets. Deepak Rao had found them wandering around the monorail station, and offered them a home and food.

Ana tried to shut out the thought of what had happened then.

She looked around. Light spilled in from a barred window set high into the wall. The window was at street level and showed only a dark patch of sky.

She sat and rubbed her bruises and the bump on the back of her head.

'Ana? Is that you?'

Her heart skipped at the sound of the voice. For a second she thought it was Ajay, and then she made out in the dimness the small shape of a young boy called Bindra. She had known Bindra for more than a year. He had worked as a shoeshine boy outside the Hilton Hotel in Old Delhi.

'Bindra? What are you doing here?'

'Last week someone stole all my brushes and polish. I had to beg in the streets. Then Rao came along and offered me a bed and work.' He paused. 'What happens now, Ana? Where am I?'

How could she begin to tell him what the future had in store? He sat in the corner and stared at her. He had two legs, two arms, and his eyes shone brightly in the little light that filtered in from outside.

'I don't know,' she whispered, not meeting his eyes. 'I don't know what happens now.'

She looked around the chamber, saw the small shapes of other children lying on the floor, asleep.

Bindra was silent for a while. 'And Ajay? Where is Ajay?'

Ana began to speak, but found that the words stuck in her throat. At last she said, 'Someone took Ajay, a friend of Rao's. I don't know where he is.'

'I'm sorry, Ana,' Bindra said. 'Maybe when Rao lets us out, maybe then you can find Ajay?'

'Maybe, Bindra,' Ana said. She watched the small boy lie down on the floor and try to sleep. She thought of the fate in store for Bindra and the other children in the chamber . . . and then wondered what Rao had planned for *her*.

Of course, she could always try to escape.

No one ever tried to escape from Deepak Rao's chamber. When he brought new children to the warehouse, he would tell them that if they tried to get away he would throw them in the river. Everyone was so frightened of being thrown into the river that they never even thought of trying to get away.

Perhaps, Ana thought, there might be a way out.

She looked up at the trapdoor, but it was too high up and in the centre of the ceiling. She would be unable to reach it.

But, if she could climb the wall she would be able to reach the barred window.

Deepak had made a mistake in letting her keep her crutch.

If she could reach the opening, push her crutch against the bars . . . just maybe she could force one out of the crumbling wall and create a gap wide enough to squeeze through.

But first she had to find a way up the wall.

Ana stood and placing her crutch carefully between the sleeping children she hopped across the chamber. She paused before the wall and ran her fingers up and down the brickwork. Some of the bricks were worn and hollowed. She would be able to push her fingers and toes into the gaps and pull herself up.

She threaded her arm through the D-shaped handle of her crutch and hung it from her shoulder, then reached up and dug her fingers between the crumbling bricks. She pulled herself up, finding a hollow with her toes. She paused, the weight of her body resting on her leg, then began again. She reached up, her fingers probing blindly for the next gap.

The noise of her climb alerted Bindra. 'What are you doing, Ana?'

'Shhh!' she hissed.

He fell silent.

She found a hand-hold, searched for another and found one, then dragged herself up the wall. Her toes found a gap and she rested, panting. She could almost reach up and touch the bars – then, she should be able to pull herself up on to the window ledge and get her breath back.

She reached out with her left hand and felt the fingers of her right slipping from their hold. In desperation she reached up and managed to grab a bar. She scrambled up the wall, snatching at another bar with her right hand and hauling herself up on to the window ledge. She sat, shaking with exhaustion, and looked down into the darkened chamber.

She stayed very still for five minutes, calming her nerves

before she began the next stage of her escape plan.

She pulled her crutch from her shoulder and poked it through the bars. She pushed with all her strength, willing the bars to shift.

She heard a sharp crack and thought at first that her crutch had broken. Then she saw that the brickwork at the base of the bars was crumbling. Almost tearful with relief, she pulled again. A bar shifted, dislodging bits of brick and cement powder. She reached out and tugged at the bar, and it came away in her hand.

She pushed her crutch out into the street and was about to follow it when she remembered Bindra and the others. She peered into the darkness. 'Bindra!' she hissed.

'Ana! What are you doing?'

'What do you think?' she called softly. 'Tell the others to climb the wall and escape!'

'No!' she heard Bindra say, fear in his voice. 'Rao will drown us if we escape! Don't go, Ana!'

'You've got to get away from here, far away so Rao won't find you!'

'I'm too afraid, Ana,' Bindra said.

'Bindra, you must escape. Please believe me. You've got to escape!'

She wanted to tell him the truth, but the truth was so terrible that he would never believe her.

'I must go,' Ana cried. 'Please, do as I say and escape!'

She pushed her shoulders through the gap. The bars pressed painfully against her ribs and shoulder blades as she squeezed through bit by bit. Halfway through she paused to regain her breath, and hoped that Deepak Rao would not choose now to open the trapdoor and find her.

She pulled herself into the street, picked up her crutch and hurried away from the warehouse, sadness in her heart at the thought of leaving Bindra and the others.

Fifteen minutes later, she arrived at the VR-bar. Even now, in the early hours, it was still open. A massive neon VR sign flashed on and off, filling the street with multicoloured light. She found a doorway across from the bar and curled herself into a tight ball.

She dozed on and off for the next couple of hours.

She awoke finally as dawn was breaking over the city. She yawned and stretched, aware of her empty stomach.

A taxi pulled up outside the VR-bar, and the well-dressed figure of a young man stepped out and paid the driver.

'Psst!' Ana called. 'Sanjay – over here!'

He looked into the windows of the buildings, as if expecting to find her there. Then he saw her waving from the doorway and ran across the road, dodging the traffic. He looked embarrassed as he glanced around the filthy doorway.

'Welcome to my world,' Ana said, remembering his words of the night before.

'I did say you could stay at my place.'

She stared at him. 'I'm fine on the streets,' she said, then changed the subject. 'What's the time?'

'Almost eight.' He noticed something in her expression. 'Is something wrong?'

'I'll tell you later,' she said. It was odd to think that while Sanjay had slept, comfortable in his bed, she had been imprisoned by Rao, had managed to escape, and had spent the rest of the night in the doorway.

A green van braked outside the VR-bar, and Deepak Rao squeezed himself from behind the driver's seat. She was aware of her heart pounding at the sight of him.

'There's Rao,' she said in a small voice, pointing.

Sanjay watched as Rao entered the bar. 'Ready, Ana? Let's go.'

She stood, gathering her crutch. As she crossed the road next to Sanjay, Ana wondered what experiences awaited her this time inside the strange world of the Web.

CHAPTER FIVE

BELLATRIX III

Deepak Rao crossed the carpeted floor of the VR-bar and stepped into one of the single booths that lined the far wall.

Sanjay led Ana to a double booth and locked the door behind them. Two couches occupied the booth, a grey Websuit lying on each. Ana sat down and pulled on the suit. The material clung to her as if it were wet. She pulled on the face mask and stared through the goggles at Sanjay.

'I'll go first,' he said. 'I'll follow Rao to whichever Webtown he enters, try to find out which site he goes to. Then I'll come back to BB and meet you there.'

He lay down and pressed the red button on his wristpad. Ana watched him, finding it hard to believe that now Sanjay would be walking around in the Web. It looked as if he were asleep and dreaming. His arms and legs twitched from time to time, and once or twice his head turned.

Ana lay back and pressed the red button on her wristpad.

Instantly, she was standing on the golden plain, the multi-coloured blocks before her under a bright blue sky. She peered down at her body. She looked like she did in the real world, except here she had two legs, and she was dressed in a simple white smock.

She looked around for Sanjay, but there was no sign of him. From time to time she saw other figures appear, fizzing into existence from nowhere before moving quickly to the coloured blocks and disappearing inside.

Then two figures appeared from a block to her left. As she watched they waved and ran across to her.

Ana stared. The figures looked for all the world like upright green frogs with domed heads, little pot-bellies and spindly legs.

'Ana,' the taller frog said in Sanjay's voice. 'Don't be alarmed, it's only me.'

'Sanjay?'

'And this is Rom,' said the taller frog. The smaller frog gave a little bow. 'Hi, Ana. How's things?'

'There's a lot of explaining to do,' said the Sanjay-frog. 'First, tap in these coordinates.' He gave her a list of numbers and letters, and she tapped them into her wristpad.

Instantly, she was aware that she had changed appearance. She looked down at her arms and legs. They were thin and green, and she had a little belly just like Sanjay and Rom.

'Welcome to the club, Ana,' Rom said. 'Don't we look just great?'

Ana had to laugh. 'What's happening, Sanjay?'

The first frog was walking towards the block. Ana and Rom joined him. 'I followed Rao to the Exploration Webtown,' Sanjay said. 'He went to a site called Bellatrix III.'

Ana frowned. 'What's that?'

'It's an imaginary planet, one of thousands the Web authorities have created and stored in the exploration system,' Sanjay explained. 'I followed Rao there and saw him meet a woman. They boarded a power boat and headed off across the sea towards an island—'

'But why are we disguised as frogs?' Ana asked.

'I'll get to that,' Sanjay said. 'While I was on Bellatrix III I noticed a lot of spiders – they're security systems that make sure we don't go where we're not supposed to. The island was one of these no go areas. I don't have the know-how to get around these systems, but guess who does? I left Bellatrix and accessed a few sites where I know Rom hangs out.'

'And I like a challenge,' Rom said.

'But why frogs?' Ana tried again.

'You'll soon find out,' Sanjay said. He linked hands with Ana and Rom and they stepped into the block.

Webtown stretched away like a glinting city of sky-scrapers, crowded with a million other Web users. For a second Ana was conscious of her guise of a frog – but then she noticed the many physical types all around her: animals of all kinds, even insects and birds, and fish that swam through the air.

Sanjay gave instructions, and Ana tapped a code into her wristpad. A second later she found herself alongside Rom and Sanjay, standing before the Bellatrix III block. The façade of the block showed an alien landscape. Hand in hand, the three frogs stepped through.

They were standing on a beach of black sand, facing a vast ocean. The water was thick and green, moving with sluggish ripples towards the shore. From time to time, whale-like creatures broke the surface of the sea, spouted geysers of green water from their blowholes, then submerged. A huge, molten red sun filled the horizon, slow-motion fountains of flame spewing from its circumference.

'It's so . . . strange,' Ana said, inadequately.

'It's the ancient planet of an ancient sun,' Sanjay said, 'near the end of its life.'

Added to the oddity of being in the Web again, the gravity of this planet was less than that of Earth. Ana had no idea how it was achieved, but she felt lighter on Bellatrix III, as if she could leap into the air and float.

She looked around her at the planet, the jungle of black trees behind her, the thick green soup of the sea. She concentrated, and felt the pressure of the Websuit against her body and the Realworld couch beneath her.

Sanjay and Rom were pointing out to sea. Ahead of them, outlined against the bloody half-circle of the sun, was the dark cone of an island.

Then Ana saw why they were disguised as frogs.

Along the beach sat a circle of small green creatures, frogs just like themselves. Pulled up on to the sands beside them was a wooden fishing boat.

'The Web authorities thought it'd be more exciting if the planet had aliens,' Sanjay explained. 'So they generated these creatures. If we go to the island disguised as aliens, then Rao and the woman might think nothing of it.'

'But first,' Rom said, 'we have to get to the island, right?' He pointed along the beach to where two hairy spiders, each one as big as a dog, ran towards them on long black legs.

Ana stepped back in fright. Rom touched her shoulder with a little green hand. 'Be careful. If they bite us, we'll find ourselves scuttled back to the VR-bar.'

The spiders halted before them, bodies bobbing up and down. 'Welcome to Bellatrix III,' the first spider piped up. 'We hope you will enjoy your visit here. Please allow us to remind you that certain features of this site are out of bounds.'

The second spider went on, 'You are welcome to explore the mainland, but do not attempt to venture across the straits to the island. Trespass will be met by increasingly severe warnings.'

Rom stepped forward. 'Outa my face, hairies,' he said, fingers working on the keyboard of his wristpad.

The fluting voice of the first spider began to protest, before it vanished along with its mate.

'How did you do that?' Ana asked.

The Rom-frog winked at her. 'Just a little sub-routine I cooked up back home in New England,' he said. 'Trouble is, when we get to the island the spiders will be bigger and fiercer, and my programs might not work as well.'

'Let's worry about that when we get there,' Sanjay said. 'Do you think the natives will mind if we borrow their fishing boat?'

'They're Web constructs,' Rom said, 'so they can't stop us. Come on.'

Ana followed her friends towards the gathering of frogs. The seated aliens seemed not to notice as Sanjay and Rom hauled their broad-bottomed boat down the beach towards the sea. Ana joined in, her feet sinking into the hot black sand as she pushed.

They jumped aboard the bobbing boat and Sanjay passed Ana and Rom a pair of oars. She had never rowed a boat before, but after watching Rom and Sanjay she soon fell into rhythm.

They made good progress through the thick soup of the sea, the lower gravity making the oars as light as cricket bats. Ana concentrated, trying to discern the lie of this 'reality'. Of course, visually and aurally it was wholly convincing – but when it came to the sensation of smell . . . Ana smiled to herself. She might have been on an alien planet in the Web, but she could still smell the familiar scents of her native India. The aroma of spiced food wafted into the VR-bar, along with the scent of joss-sticks, cow dung and petrol fumes.

Five minutes later Ana saw her first ghost.

She was sweating beneath the heat of the sun when the face of a boy appeared, floating in the air beside the boat. His expression was pained. His mouth opened but no words sounded.

Ana screamed.

Sanjay turned to her. 'What's wrong?'

She pointed out to sea. 'There . . . There, I thought I saw . . . a face – the face of a young boy.'

But there was nothing in the sky now.

Sanjay looked at Rom, who shrugged. 'Could be a Web-ghost,' the American said. 'Don't be alarmed. They happen all the time – stray machine memories bleeding into site programs. They look frightening, but they're only virtual illusions, OK?'

Ana didn't understand half of his explanation, but she nodded anyway and said that she was fine.

She concentrated on rowing, and they made steady progress towards the island. It rose steeply from the calm waters of the ocean, its sides covered with a forest of trees like burnt matchsticks. On the highest point of the island was a solid, square building constructed of red bricks, dark against the light of the setting sun.

A beach of black sand came into view and they rowed all the faster. Ana kept a look out for spiders patrolling the foreshore, but the island seemed still and quiet in the twilight.

The keel scraped the shelving sands of the shallows. Rom and Sanjay leaped out and pulled the boat up the beach.

Ana stepped on to the hot sand and stared back at the mainland. She looked up into the sky. The light was failing fast. 'How will we be able to row back in the darkness?' she asked.

Rom stared at her, his big mouth split wide as he laughed out loud.

Sanjay smiled. 'Think about it, Ana.'

She felt herself blushing. 'What? I don't see—'

Sanjay held up his right arm and pointed to his wristpad. 'We don't have to row back to leave Bellatrix III,' he explained. 'All we do to get back to the VR-bar is hit the scuttle button. OK?'

'Ah-cha,' Ana whispered. 'I see.'

Rom strode up the beach and peered into the forest of blackened trees. 'I can see a footpath,' he called back. 'I guess it leads up to the house.'

They left the beach and climbed the path through the trees, Rom leading the way, Ana second and Sanjay behind her. The eerie silence was broken from time to time by the quick chirping of birds. Ana saw dark shapes leaping with silent agility through the tree-tops.

'Careful,' Rom warned suddenly. 'We have company!'

Ana's heart jumped. She looked all around her, unable to spot the danger. Sanjay pointed up the path.

A spider almost as tall as Ana straddled the path before them. Its great hairy body bobbed on the sprung suspension of its legs. Two eye-stalks bent to regard them.

'You are contravening Web-codes,' the spider said in mechanical tones. 'Please turn about and leave the island. Failure to obey this command will lead to summary expulsion.'

Ana gripped Sanjay's arm. 'What is it saying?'

'It said that if we don't go away it'll bite us out of the Web.'

Rom was tapping frantically on his wristpad. 'I'm finding it hard to shift,' he called out. 'Pick up a big stick each and hit it if it tries to bite you.'

The spider advanced one step. Rom backed off, still tapping. Ana and Sanjay stepped backwards too, looking around them for suitable weapons. Ana saw a hefty branch on the forest floor and picked it up. Sanjay found a shorter club and gave it a practice swing.

The spider bent its legs, as if preparing itself to jump at Rom. Instead, it scurried forward, trying to catch Rom off guard while he was busy with his wristpad. Sanjay dashed past Rom and swung his club with all his might but narrowly missed. The spider scurried backwards, hissing.

'Take care, Ana,' Sanjay called to her. 'The Web might be make believe, but we can still feel pain.'

Ana was aware of her limbs shaking in fear. She tried to tell herself that all this was an illusion, that really she was lying on a couch back in New Delhi. But her brain was convinced that she was on Bellatrix III in the disguise of an alien frog and being attacked by an overgrown spider.

The spider advanced again, jumped at Rom in an attempt to bite him. Sanjay swung his club again and this time made contact. One of the spider's legs snapped and trailed uselessly along the ground as the spider backed off up the path.

'There!' Rom cried in triumph. He stabbed a finger down on his keyboard, and the injured spider dissolved in a swirl of colour and disappeared.

Sanjay stood panting. 'That one was too close for comfort. It almost had you, Rom.'

'I was doing everything I knew. Once it was weakened, I could override its defences. You OK, Ana?'

She nodded. 'Ah-cha,' she said. 'I'm fine.'

They began climbing again. The trees soon thinned out, and they passed from the forest to stand on the edge of a sloping sweep of grass. High above them, its lighted windows looking down like watchful eyes, a red-brick building stood dark against the evening sky.

Ana saw movement to her right. She turned. In the air before her she made out the indistinct shape of a floating face. She stared at the ghost, opened her mouth and tried to scream.

The ghost gained solidity, became the brown face of a young Indian boy. Its lips moved, forming silent words. It seemed to be pleading, begging her to help.

Then, as quickly as it had appeared, it vanished into the gathering dusk.

Ana turned to Sanjay and Rom. They stood very still, staring at where the apparition had been.

At last she found her voice. 'I-I know who it was,' she said. 'A year ago a boy called Dilli— Deepak Rao took him out begging one morning, and Dilli never came back.'

'It's OK, Ana,' Sanjay soothed. 'It's OK.'

'But it isn't OK!' Ana cried. 'What happened to him – what's happening to all the children that Rao has given to the woman?'

She thought of her brother, and pain clutched at her heart like an evil fist.

CHAPTER SIX

THE HOUSE OF
STOLEN CHILDREN

'We'll go round to the back of the house,' Rom said. 'It's too open here – they'd see us if we tried to get near. Follow me.'

He led the way through the bushes, up the hill and then along the side of the house. Ana told herself that she should not fear for her own safety – whatever happened, Rao and the woman could not harm her. All she had to do to escape was hit the scuttle button on her wristpad.

But she could worry about what might be happening to Ajay.

They emerged from the bushes at the back of the house. Before them was a flat lawn overlooking the ocean. The lawn was enclosed by a high wire-mesh fence. Imprisoned behind the fence were perhaps a dozen young children. As Ana stared, she realized that she recognized many of them – Sita, Nazreen, Parveen. They were dressed in identical white trousers and shirts, and of course they were not wearing wristpads.

She turned to Sanjay. 'But why imprison the children behind the fence?' she asked. 'Surely the island is prison enough.'

Sanjay shrugged. 'Maybe the woman doesn't want the kids seen by Web users on the mainland. What she's doing here isn't exactly legal, Ana.'

She moved to the fence and clutched the wire. 'Ajay!' she cried. 'Ajay, are you there?'

Something moved to her right. She turned. A spider the size of a barrel scurried towards her. She backed off until she bumped into Sanjay. Rom stepped forward, fingering his wristpad.

The spider advanced. As before, Sanjay leaped forward and swung his club at the spider. This one was faster than the first and leaped back out of reach.

Ana yelled at Rom and Sanjay. Advancing along the side of the fence was yet another spider, scurrying towards them on long, nimble legs.

Rom looked over his shoulder. 'OK, I think it's time to retreat, guys. Back into the bushes.'

Ana was about to step into the cover of the bushes when she saw a small figure among the children on the lawn. The boy was walking towards the fence, his head cocked as if he had heard a familiar voice.

'Ajay!' Ana cried. She ran to the fence again. 'Ajay, I'm here!'

Ajay heard her, and a smile transformed his face.

'Ana!' Rom called out. 'Come on!'

Sanjay and Rom were already in the bushes. Sanjay was beating off a spider with his club.

'I can't leave Ajay!' Ana cried.

'You can't do anything for him here!' Rom tried to reason with her. 'Remember, he's not really here on the island – he's somewhere out there in Realworld.'

'But I can't just leave him!' she sobbed.

'Ana!'

She turned at Sanjay's scream. A spider was running towards her with high, quick steps, its mandibles clacking like castanets. She stumbled backwards and fell, then scrambled on all fours towards the bushes. Sanjay grabbed her arm and pulled her into the bushes. Rom was still tapping codes into his keypad. As Ana watched, the first spider exploded in a swirl of multicoloured pixels and vanished. There was no time to feel relief. The second spider darted towards them, jaws working.

Rom tapped desperately. He called over his shoulder. 'Might as well press your scuttle buttons, guys. This is the end of the road.'

The spider darted forward and leaped at Rom. Its mouth found his arm, and Rom cried out in pain. Instantly, the frog who had been Rom dissolved in a whirlwind of a million green bubbles and disappeared as if he had never existed.

Sanjay cried out and swung at the spider with his club. The impact snapped three of its legs. It stumbled around in a drunken circle, attempting to steady itself and charge at Sanjay. As it came, he stepped forward and like a cricket batsman swiped at the spider's body. He made full contact and swept the creature high into the air.

'Let's scuttle, Ana,' Sanjay said. 'We can't do anything without Rom here to help us. It won't be long before another spider shows itself.'

'No! I've got to talk to Ajay!'

'But think about it, Ana. You can't do anything. He's not really here, remember?'

'But he might know where he is in the real world!' Ana yelled at Sanjay. 'Don't you see? If he knows where he is in Delhi, then maybe I can find him!'

Without waiting for his reply, Ana ran from the cover of the bushes and approached the fence. She told herself that two minutes was all she needed, two minutes to question her brother, find out where the woman in the Mercedes had taken him.

'Ajay!' she called, fingers clutching the wire of the fence.

The little barefoot boy moved towards the source of the

sound, his head held to one side and his sightless eyes staring straight ahead.

'Ajay, over here. Quickly!' She looked towards the house, but there was no sign of life at any of the windows.

Ajay stopped at the fence and reached out. Ana poked her fingers through the wire and touched his hand. He pressed his face to the fence and Ana kissed him. The skin of his cheek was warm, just as she remembered it in real life.

'Ana, where am I? What did they do to me?'

'You're in the Web, Ajay.'

'The Web?' He looked bemused, even though he knew all about the Web in theory. 'I'm really in the Web? I wondered. I was taken away in a car, Ana. Taken into a house and made to wear a tight suit. Then I found myself in a different place. I was suddenly outside. It was so hot, even hotter than home. And the smells – I could still smell India. I wondered . . . I wondered if I was in the Web.' He shook his head. 'But why? What are they doing to us?'

'I don't know, Ajay. Listen, I need to know where the woman took you. Do you understand? I can't help you now – I'm in the Web just like you. I need to know where you are in real life. Where did the woman take you, Ajay? *Which part of Delhi?*'

Ajay frowned, then shook his head. 'I don't know. We . . . we drove for ten minutes after I was picked up. We stopped and I was taken from the car, across grass and into a building. But I don't know where it was, Ana.'

'Don't worry. I'll get you out. Honestly, I'll get you out somehow.'

'I've been in here a long time, Ana. I feel sick all the time. But some of the others, Sharma and Parveen – they've been here for months, made to stay in here and never let out!' He made a vague gesture behind him, and Ana saw two children sitting in the middle of the lawn, clutching their legs and rocking back and forth in distress.

Ana heard a sound behind her. She turned, fearing the attack of another spider. Instead, Sanjay pushed through the bushes.

Ajay jumped. 'Who is that?'

'It's OK, Ajay. I'm with a friend.'

'Ana,' Sanjay hissed urgently. 'Quick, get down!'

Before she could protest, Sanjay grabbed her arm and dragged her into the concealment of the bushes. As she squatted and peered through the leaves at the house, the back door opened and two figures stepped out on to the lawn.

The woman had a shock of bleached blonde hair and wore the same short silver dress that her older self wore in the real world. A younger, slimmer version of Deepak Rao strolled across the lawn beside her.

Ajay hooked his fingers through the wire of the fence. 'Ana? Ana, where are you?'

'Ajay,' Ana hissed, 'please be quiet!'

Rao and the woman walked at a leisurely pace around the lawn, chatting. They approached the fence where Ajay stood and paused behind him. Ana ducked further into the cover of the bush.

'. . . This child has only recently been introduced into the Web,' the woman was saying. 'So of course the effects of long-term exposure have yet to manifest themselves.'

Rao nodded. 'Very interesting . . .' he murmured.

The woman glanced at him. 'You don't approve? Let me tell you that I see very little difference between what I am doing here and your own operations out there in Realworld.'

'Come, come. I see a – please excuse the pun – a world of difference.'

'How so?' the woman snapped. 'You use children to your own ends, manipulating them for your personal benefit, and I have the honesty to admit that I do the same.'

'But permit me to point out that I happen to look after my children. Yes, I take a percentage of their earnings, but I also provide them with shelter.'

'And I initiate my children to the wonders of the Web,' the woman responded. 'By the way – you do have the children you promised me yesterday?'

Rao nodded. 'Safe and secure and to be delivered to you at midday. Oh, and for a little extra I can even supply you with another child if you wish – Ajay's sister.'

Ana stiffened, realizing what Rao was talking about. Bindra and the other children in the chamber – they were all destined to be delivered to the woman at noon.

'Excellent,' the woman said.

Rao paused, a finger to his lips in a gesture Ana had seen many times before. 'Perhaps, now that you have taken me into your confidence, you will tell me what it is exactly that you are hoping to gain from these . . . these *experiments?*'

The woman stared out across the ocean. Her face took on a calculating look. 'Very well, Rao . . .' she said, but her words were lost as she began strolling away across the lawn towards the house, Rao in eager attendance.

Sanjay grabbed Ana's arm. 'What did he mean, he can give you to the woman?'

Ana looked at Sanjay's frog face. 'Last night he captured me, threw me into the chamber. I managed to get away and meet you. But he obviously still thinks I'm imprisoned—'

'Ana?' Ajay called from the fence. 'Ana, are you still there?'

'I'm here, Ajay – but I'm leaving now. I promise that I'll see you very soon.'

Ajay smiled. 'Please hurry,' he whispered, tears falling down his cheeks.

'I'll get you away from here, Ajay,' Ana said.

Sanjay shook his head. 'But how can you get them out?' he whispered. 'We don't even know where they are in Realworld!'

Ana looked up at her brother. 'Bye, Ajay. I'm going now.' She turned to Sanjay. 'See you back at the VR-bar.'

She hit the scuttle button.

Ana lay on the Web-couch in the double booth, blinking up at the ceiling and wondering if the events on the island had really happened. They seemed so real, and yet at the same time so fantastic. Then she remembered Ajay and the tears on his face.

She knew what she had to do. She had to act fast and make sure Sanjay would help her.

She struggled into a sitting position and quickly peeled off her Websuit. Beside her, Sanjay was sitting up. He seemed to be moving in slow motion, and Ana realized how drab the colours of the real world were after the cinema gloss of the Web.

Sanjay pulled off his face mask. 'You didn't answer my question, Ana. How can we get the children out of there—'

'Think about it, Sanjay. It's very simple, really.'

'Go to the police?'

Ana nearly laughed. 'The police? Is that what you'd do?' She shook her head. 'For all I know, the woman pays the police to take no notice of what she's doing. I wouldn't trust the police with a dirty rupee.'

'You have a better plan?' he asked, pulling off his Websuit.

She stood up, found her crutch and fitted it under her

arm. 'Of course. I'm going back to the chamber where Rao had me imprisoned.'

Sanjay stared at her. 'You can't!'

'Why not? Didn't you hear him – he said he would deliver me and the other kids to the woman at noon.'

'But what good would that do? You'd be locked in the Web like the rest of them!'

Ana nodded, staring straight at Sanjay. 'Of course, and that's why I need your help.'

He shook his head. 'But what can I do?'

'Go back to Bellatrix III at noon, cross to the island. I'll be on the lawn, near the fence where Ajay was standing.'

'I don't understand how that will help—'

'Listen to me, Sanjay. When Rao takes me and the others to where the woman is in the real world, I'll remember the route, ah-cha? When I see you on the island, I'll tell you where I am in Delhi.'

Sanjay spread his arms in a defeated gesture. 'What good will that do, Ana? So I'll know where you are in Realworld. What do I do then? The place will be guarded. How do I get in on my own? Have you thought about that?'

Ana stared at him, considering. 'Perhaps you can do something to attract the attention of the guards, then enter the house and get us out of the Web.'

'Like what? You make it sound so easy—'

'I don't know . . .' Ana said, frustrated. 'But you've got to create some kind of diversion.'

Sanjay was shaking his head.

'Have you got a better idea?' Ana cried. 'At least my plan is better than nothing!'

'I'm not suggesting that we do nothing.'

'Then what are you suggesting, wise guy? Come on, let's hear your plan.' She stared at him, angry.

He just sat on the edge of the couch, staring down at his fingers. 'I don't know, Ana. I just don't know. I've never been in a situation like this before.'

'Then we'll follow my plan?'

'It's just too risky, Ana.'

'Are you frightened the spiders might bite you, Sanjay? Are you frightened you'll be caught by the woman's guards?'

Sanjay looked up, shook his head. 'I'm not frightened that anything will happen to me,' he said. 'I'm frightened that something will happen to you.'

They stared at each other across the small room. The silence stretched. Ana suddenly wanted to hug this privileged little Brahmin boy for what he'd just said.

The odd thing was that she would gladly go back and imprison herself in the chamber, but she could not find the courage to tell Sanjay how much she liked him.

'I've got to help Ajay and the others, Sanjay,' she said at last. 'You saw the second ghost. The woman must be doing terrible things to the children – even more terrible than what Rao would have done to them—'

She stopped there.

'What do you mean?' Sanjay asked. 'What would Rao have done to them?'

Ana raised the stump of her right leg, so that it pointed at him. He looked away, embarrassed.

'I was lying when I told you that I'd had a monorail accident,' she said.

He still could not meet her eyes. 'What happened?'

Her voice wavered as she told him. 'Rao picked us up off the streets, took us back to the warehouse and locked us in the chamber with some other children. Then he took us out one by one. He . . . he injected paraffin into my right knee. It went bad, and he took me to the hospital, pretending to be my father. The doctor said that they must cut off the leg to save my life, and of course Rao agreed.

'I can't remember the next few days. The pain was more terrible than anything . . . Rao kept me in the chamber until I got better, then let me out. Then I saw what Rao had done to Ajay.' She paused there, waited five seconds before going on. 'He'd blinded him.

'Then Rao took us out on to the streets of Delhi to beg for money from people like you, and he took the money and bought himself all those gold rings.'

Sanjay was shaking his head, whispering, 'I'm sorry, Ana. I'm so sorry.'

'So do you see why I have to try and save Ajay and the other kids? Rao does terrible things to the children in his care, but what terrible things is the woman going to do to them?'

She gripped her crutch and moved to the door of the booth. 'Will you help me, Sanjay?'

He nodded. 'Ah-cha, Ana. I'll help you.'

Ana smiled at him and left the booth.

She limped from the VR-bar into the street busy with pedestrians and cars, once again just another cripple among many. She made her way to Rao's warehouse and tried to shut her mind to the dangers she would face over the next few hours. She thought only of Ajay, and how wonderful it would be to be with him again. It made the threat of danger seem bearable.

She came to the barred window of the underground chamber and crouched down. She lowered her crutch through the gap, and then squeezed through after it. She hung from the bars, her knee scraping against the wall, then let herself drop. She found her crutch and sat against the wall.

Bindra and another child were watching her, eyes wide in disbelief.

Ana smiled at them. 'It's OK,' she said. 'It's OK. I've come back to help you.'

Her heart beating like a snake-charmer's drum, Ana closed her eyes and waited.

CHAPTER SEVEN

THE QUEEN OF EVIL

Ana must have fallen asleep . . .

She was awoken by a loud noise. She looked up. A patch of light appeared in the ceiling as the trapdoor was opened. The other children in the chamber stirred and sat up groggily. Bindra rubbed his eyes, looked across at Ana with a worried expression. She smiled to reassure him.

A ladder dropped into the chamber and a face appeared in the square of light above. Deepak Rao stared down at them. 'Up, up! Quickly now!'

The children stood and moved to the ladder. Ana pushed herself upright on her crutch and limped across to the foot of it. She waited until she was the last one in the chamber, then hooked her crutch on to her shoulder, took hold of the ladder with both hands, and hopped up the rungs one at a time.

Deepak Rao and Rajiv the strong man were waiting beside the van, its back doors open to receive the children. One by one they climbed inside. Ana joined them. Rajiv locked the doors and sat in the front seat beside Rao. The engine coughed into life and seconds later they were motoring from the warehouse and down the street thronged with daytime crowds.

'Where are we going?' a little girl asked in a frightened whisper.

'Don't worry,' Ana told her. 'We'll be all together. That's the most important thing.'

Bindra sat beside her, staring at her with big, curious eyes. 'Do you really know where we're going, Ana?'

'We are going to a big house on an island,' she said. 'Now don't be afraid.'

She turned her attention to the front, and stared through the windscreen between Rao and Rajiv.

They were heading south. They circled the big round-about of Connaught Place packed with traffic, the humid air blue with petrol fumes. On the sides of the street, stall-holders sold fruit and vegetables, onion bhajis and pakoras, bottles of cola and sugar cane juice. Ana saw Begum's foodstall, where she and Ajay had sometimes eaten break-fast when the begging had gone well.

They turned down Janpath, a long, wide road jammed with stalls selling books, Indian artifacts, and the latest electrical equipment. Soon the stalls gave way to expensive, multi-storey hotels where Ana and Ajay had sometimes begged from foreign tourists. They were heading towards the select suburbs of New Delhi where many countries had their embassies and consulates, and where the rich owned massive houses set in lawns as vast and perfect as cricket pitches.

They passed the Indian Museum and turned right along Raj Path. The parliament buildings came into sight, then disappeared as the van turned left and continued south. Ana felt a knot of apprehension tighten in her stomach. She had been so confident all along – but what would happen if she could not tell Sanjay where they were, or if Sanjay failed to turn up on the island? There was so much that might go wrong.

No, she told herself, everything *will* go to plan. It *had* to. She could not imagine what might happen if her plan failed.

The van turned left, into a district of leafy suburbs. She was in an area of the city new to her. She leaned forward and peered out, staring at the nameplates on the street corners as they passed. She memorized the name of every street.

They turned again. Ana caught a brief glimpse of the nameplate. Himachal Boulevard, she repeated to herself. The van slowed, and Ana felt a glow of triumph in her chest. Himachal Boulevard, off Patel Marg—

They turned into a gravelled driveway flanked by trees. Some of the children, lulled to sleep by the motion of the van, now woke up as it slowed. They peered ahead, curious. Ana looked around for any sign of security guards, but saw none.

Then she stared through the windscreen at the house standing in the middle of a large lawn and surrounded by trees.

The house was big and square, and built of dark brick.

It was an identical copy of the house on the island on Bellatrix III. Or rather, she corrected herself, the other way around. The house on the island was an identical copy of this one.

She told herself that Sanjay would be able to locate the house without any difficulty . . . just so long as he made it to the island.

The van drove around to the rear of the house. Ana half expected to see a caged lawn full of children, but of course the children were imprisoned in the Web.

In the real world, they would be somewhere in the house.

The van jerked to a halt and Rao and Rajiv climbed out. The back doors swung open and Ana jumped down, followed by the others.

'Up the steps!' Rao shouted. 'Quickly now!'

A hand dropped on to her shoulder. 'Not you, Ana.'

She felt her stomach turn in sickening disappointment.

Rao turned her to face him with a rough hand. He lifted her chin, squeezing her cheeks with brutal fingers. His gold rings winked in the sunlight.

'I'm sorry to see you go, little one,' Rao said. 'You've been a faithful servant over the years, but then you spoilt yourself by running away. What choice do I have, little one, if I can no longer trust you?'

She squirmed out of his grip. 'Let me go!' She put all her hatred into an unblinking stare.

Rao laughed. 'You'll soon wish you'd never run away. When you've seen what lies ahead, life with me will seem like paradise. Now go!'

She felt relief that she would be allowed to join the others after all, but at the same time his words filled her with fear.

She limped up the steps and into the house, hurrying to catch up.

Rajiv led the children through the darkened house, followed by Deepak Rao. They passed down a long corridor and up a flight of narrow stairs. At last they came to a pair of double doors. The strong man knocked, waited five seconds and then opened the door. Ana peered inside.

She thought at first that it was the throne room of a palace. It had a marble floor, a red carpet stretching the length of the room, and at the far end the throne itself.

Then she saw that it was not a throne at all, but an invalid carriage. The two men standing on either side of the carriage were not courtiers, Ana saw now, but medics.

And the woman sitting in the carriage was no queen, but someone so old that all life seemed to have fled from her bent and twisted body.

Ana paused with the other children on the threshold of the room, too terrified to enter.

The woman lifted a stick-thin arm and beckoned. A command like a dying breath sounded faintly. 'Come . . .'

Deepak Rao pushed Ana in the back, and she led the other children into the room and down the red carpet towards the woman in the invalid carriage.

'The children, ma'am,' Rao said.

Ana stared at the woman's white face, covered with wrinkles like paper screwed into a ball. What made the old woman's appearance all the more ghastly, Ana saw, was the short silver dress – it was as if she was desperately trying to regain the long gone days of her youth.

Watery grey eyes peered at Ana. The woman made a feeble gesture with her right hand. 'Come closer, girl,' she croaked to Ana.

Trembling, Ana took one step towards the carriage.

Then she saw the tubes twisting from beneath the seat of the carriage. Like hungry snakes they were attached to the woman's flesh at her neck and her wrists, but these snakes were the colour of pumping blood – the same colour as the ruby ring on her left hand.

'Don't be alarmed, girl. I, like yourself, am human – though I scarcely appear so now.' The woman cocked her head to one side, regarding Ana. 'Are you horrified by what you see, girl? Come on, the truth. I want the truth!'

Ana opened her mouth, stammered, 'I-I—'

The woman interrupted. 'Well, girl, I will tell you that *I* am truly horrified every morning when I inspect myself in the mirror. What do I see but someone ravaged by disease and the treacherous advance of the years! I was once young like you, young and pretty and full of health . . . but where do the years go to, girl? How is it possible for the years, so everlastingly long in childhood, to go so fast? It's a tragedy that one must age and grow feeble, and leave behind for ever the days of one's youth.'

The woman gestured again. 'Come closer, girl. Closer!'

Ana moved closer.

A claw reached out, and cold fingers took her chin. Ana thought that she would rather have had Deepak Rao gripping her with his cruel fingrs.

'Such youth,' the woman marvelled. 'Do you understand what a precious gift you possess? But no, of course you don't. One never appreciates a possession until it is no more. Do you know what death is, girl? Do you fear it?'

Ana tried to shake her head, but the woman's cold fingers prevented the movement.

'No, of course you don't! You hardly know the meaning of the word!' She pushed Ana away and turned her attention to the other children who watched her in horror.

'For years I have stared death in the face, waited for it to come quietly in the night and carry me away.' She shook her head. 'But no more! My lost youth is within reach, thanks to you beautiful children . . .' She collapsed back into her chair, breathless.

The medics bent and busied themselves around her, administering injections, taking her pulse. After a minute she seemed to gain strength.

'Rajiv!' she called.

The strong man stepped forward. 'Ma'am.'

'Take them away!'

As Ana was led from the room, she heard the old woman say: 'And now, Mr Rao, the small matter of your payment . . .'

Rajiv and the medics hurried Ana and the children along the corridor to a room at the opposite end of the house. One of the medics unlocked the door with a key on a chain. The room beyond was gloomy, but even so Ana made out the shapes of a dozen or more Web-couches.

'Inside,' Rajiv said.

Ana limped into the room with the other children, staring around her at the machinery and computers banked along the walls. Even though she had known what to expect, the sight of the small children in the grey suits, each one bound in place on a Web-couch, filled her with panic. She looked for Ajay, but all the children looked alike in the Websuits.

She noticed that some of the children struggled against the straps that bound them down, twisting and turning like sleepers suffering nightmares. She remembered Ajay telling her that a few of the children had been held in the Web for months.

Empty Web-couches waited at the far end of the room. The medics sorted the children into groups of two or three, according to their size, and led them across to the couches. They ordered the children to put on the Websuits.

Bindra began to cry. 'What's happening, Ana? What are they doing to us?'

Ana smiled bravely. 'Don't worry. We won't be harmed. We'll find ourselves in a . . . a new world. And we'll be together. OK?'

Bindra pursed his lips and nodded as he pulled on the suit.

Ana laid her crutch on the floor, pulled on the suit and stretched out on the couch. The medics passed around face masks and goggles, and ordered the children to put them on. As Ana did so, she reached automatically for the wristpad – but of course these suits were without the devices.

The first medic moved from couch to couch, strapping down the children. He arrived at Ana's couch and fastened her so that she could not move.

The second medic crossed to a computer terminal and pressed a series of keys. Ana's vision was filled with darkness.

Then she could see again. She found that she could sit up. For a second she thought that nothing had happened, that she was still in the same room.

Then she noticed that the medics had disappeared, and that the computers were no longer in the room. Red sunlight slanted in through the long window to her right. She sat up and saw that she was not on the couch, but sitting on a bed. She was dressed in a white shirt and trousers, like all the other children she had seen on the island earlier – and once again she had two legs.

The other children were climbing to their feet, looking about them in bewilderment.

Ana jumped from the bed, lighter now in the gravity of Bellatrix III, and ran to the window. She gazed down on to the lawn, and there by the fence was Ajay.

CHAPTER EIGHT

THE GHOST IN THE WEB

'Where are we?' a little girl cried.

The children climbed from the beds and looked around in fear.

'Don't be afraid,' Ana said. 'We're in the Web. We'll be OK if we all keep together. Now hold hands and we'll go down to the lawn.'

She led the way from the room and down the stairs, marvelling again at the sensation of walking on two legs. The house was deserted, with no sign of the woman or the medics. The children followed her timidly.

She found the door leading to the back garden. It stood ajar, and through it she could see children wandering aimlessly around the lawn, standing still and gazing out across the vast ocean, or sitting and rocking back and forth in distress. Ajay stood by the fence, facing the bushes where just a few hours ago she and Sanjay had hidden. She ran across to him.

'Ajay!'

He turned, an expression of disbelief on his face. 'Ana? Ana, is it really you?'

Unable to speak, she moved to her brother and took him in her arms. He was as she remembered him from the real world, the same small warm bundle, the brother she had looked after and loved for the six years of his life.

'Ana, how did you get here? Did she . . . did the woman get you too?'

She sat him down on the lawn, and lowered herself beside him, holding his hand and saying, 'It's a long story, Ajay. I had to let the woman capture me. I have a plan. A friend out in the real world is helping me. With luck we'll be able to get everyone out of here.'

She looked around the lawn. The children who had been imprisoned here for a while were talking to the new arrivals. Some knew each other from the real world. They hugged and exchanged what little information they possessed.

Some children, those sitting on the ground and rocking back and forth, were not aware of the latest arrivals. They stared into space with pained expressions.

Ana squeezed her brother's fingers. 'Ajay, do you know what's happening here? Do any of the other children know?'

He shook his head. 'We've talked about it. When we go back to our rooms to sleep at night, we try to work out what is happening. Why the woman is doing this to us. But, Ana, *nothing* is happening. That's the awful thing. Nothing happens, and there's nothing to do. The children who've been here for longer than me say that every day is the same. We will just wait here until—' He stopped, staring blindly into space.

'Until what, Ajay?'

'At first, it seems a good place. It is warm and comfortable. No one harms us. We don't have to beg or work. We are fed once a day. I feel a tube enter my mouth and then my tummy feels full.' He shrugged. 'Some children say that they like it here, at first.'

'And then?'

'And then . . .' He frowned, shaking his head. 'Strange things happen to the children. Come, I'll show you.'

Ajay stood and held out his hand. 'Can you see Parveen, Ana? She sits all day and rocks back and forth.'

'She's over by the steps.' Ana took Ajay's hand and walked him over to where the little girl rocked, humming to herself.

Ajay squatted before her. 'Parveen, Ana is here.'

The girl stared through Ana and went on rocking back and forth, her hands on her knees.

Ana reached out and touched her arm. 'Parveen, can you tell me how long you've been here?'

The girl stopped rocking. She looked at Ana, but her gaze seemed far away, as if she were seeing not Ana but some other world.

'A long, long time,' Parveen said. 'So long that I am no longer really here.'

'Parveen, what do you mean?'

The girl shook her head, as if she found her situation hard to describe. 'I see you, I see the house and the lawn, but I also see . . . other things.' She stopped talking and began rocking back and forth again.

Ana took the girl's hand and squeezed. 'Parveen, I want to help you. I want to get you away from here and back to the real world. Tell me, what other things do you see?'

Parveen frowned. 'Other worlds . . . hundreds and thousands of other worlds, all on top of each other. It is like . . . like watching a thousand holo-ads all at once. Soon, I will leave here for ever and travel through all those other worlds.'

'How do you know this?'

'Because they have told me.'

Ana blinked. 'They? Who are *they*?'

'They,' the girl repeated. 'The others. The other children who were here, but are no longer here.'

Ana shook her head. 'I don't understand,' she said in a whisper.

Ajay said, 'I think she means the ghosts.'

'The ghosts . . .' Ana repeated in a small voice. She recalled the ghostly head she had seen on the island, the face of Dilli floating in the air.

'Parveen,' she said. 'Is Dilli a ghost?'

The girl nodded. 'Dilli and Shazeen and Babu. They all live in the other worlds, now, and soon I will join them.'

Ajay took Ana's hand. 'The ghosts sometimes come and shout to us. They need our help.'

'Parveen,' Ana said. 'Do you know why the woman is doing this to us? Do you know what is happening?'

But Parveen just shook her head and continued rocking back and forth, back and forth.

Ana turned to her brother. 'When do the ghosts come, Ajay?'

He shrugged. 'I hear them all the time, calling to us. They live in the hills around the house.'

Ana looked through the fence, recalling the ghosts she had seen earlier, Dilli on the hillside and the other floating head she had encountered above the sea.

Maybe, if she could find another ghost and question it about what was happening here . . .

Ana left Parveen and walked Ajay over to the fence. She stood and looked down the hillside at the green ocean, across which Sanjay would soon be coming – she hoped.

A thought occurred to her. Why wait until Sanjay reached the house? She would make his task easier by getting out of the compound and walking down the hillside to meet him on the beach. That way, he would not have to do battle with the spiders that patrolled the island. She could tell him the location of the house in the real world and he could scuttle and do something to rescue them.

'Ajay, can we get out of this cage?'

'There is a gap under the fence near the house. Other

children got out and tried to get away. But they found we are on an island a long way from the mainland . . . so they could not escape.'

'Do you know how often the woman comes here?' Ana asked.

'The others say that she arrives every evening. She moves around the lawn, talking to the children like Parveen about what they can see.'

Ana nodded. 'That gives me plenty of time. Ajay, listen to me. I'm going away for a short while, ah-cha? But I'll be back soon.'

Ajay looked suddenly frightened. 'Ana, promise me you'll come back!' He reached out, found her hand and gripped it.

'I'll be back. I need to meet a friend. It's very important.'

They stood and Ajay led her to a section of the fence in the shadow of the house, and then stopped. Ana saw a semi-circular gap in the fence where it had been pulled up.

She said goodbye to Ajay and squirmed through. She stood in the sunlight on the side of the hill, and felt as if she had made the first step on the journey to freedom.

She hurried down the hillside, through the bushes and across the open grass in front of the house, and then along the steep path through the blackened trees.

A spider appeared suddenly on the path before her. She halted, the sight of the hairy monster filling her with fright.

As she stared, she realized that the spider seemed unaware of her. It was looking the other way, its eye-stalks bent towards the coast.

She recalled what Rom had told her, that a spider's bite would scuttle them from the Web.

What would happen if the spider bit her now? Would she find herself in the woman's house in Delhi? If so, then she would be able to help the others to escape without having to wait for Sanjay.

It was too much to hope for, of course.

She stepped forward and called to the spider. It took no notice of her. She reached out and touched the hairy monstrosity, its furry warmth beneath her fingertips making her shudder.

The spider moved, scurrying off into the trees to her left.

Ana continued down the path.

Two minutes later she saw movement to her right. She turned quickly.

A disembodied head bobbed between the trunks of the nearest trees, staring at her. With a sickening feeling in the pit of her stomach, she recognized the face of the boy she had known as Dilli.

The floating head moved its lips, and Ana thought she heard the faintest whiper. 'Ana, please . . . help me.'

'I . . .' she began. 'How . . . how can I help you?'

'I too was like you, Ana. Then she caught me, imprisoned me in the house in the Web. I was there for many months, Ana, slowly fading away. Now I am no longer . . . *real*. I can't feel, or move or experience as I did before. There are more of us who live like this in the Web, the children who the woman captured and imprisoned.'

Ana called out, 'But why is she doing this to us?'

'We do not know why. We are ghosts, being kept alive by the woman . . .' The face was fading away, its words becoming faint.

'Please . . . Please help us!'

Seconds before the floating head vanished, Ana stepped forward. 'I will try!' she called. 'I promise, Dilli, I will do my best . . .'

She turned and hurried down the path towards the coast.

She came to a clearing in the trees and looked across the

bay to the mainland. There was no sign of the rowing boat. She willed Sanjay to hurry up. She wondered how long Parveen had before she, like Dilli and the other children, became a ghost in the Web.

Ana was about to begin the descent again when she saw movement on the black sands of the beach. She stared. Six black spiders ran towards the sea, lifting their legs high as if scurrying over hot coals. They paused by the water, staring out across the ocean as if they somehow knew that Sanjay was on his way.

At that very second, Ana saw the rowing boat appear around the headland and make for the beach. Two small frog-figures sat side by side, rowing with all their strength.

Ana called to them and waved, then bounded along the path, taking great leaps in the lighter gravity.

She came to the beach as one of the frog-figures jumped out of the boat and dragged it through the shallows. The other frog stood in the prow of the boat, holding an oar ready to hit out at the waiting spiders.

'Sanjay, Rom!' Ana yelled, waving as she ran towards the sea.

Then the spiders attacked, swarming through the breakers towards the boat. The two frogs jumped out and fought with the spiders, knocking the creatures from the water with fierce blows of the oars. Sanjay, the taller frog, spun in a mad circle, his oar like a propeller as it scythed down the advancing spiders. If Ana had had time to think about what was happening, she might have noticed how comical the contest appeared – two giant frogs duelling with half a dozen overgrown spiders.

But all she knew was that she had to reach Sanjay before one of the spiders bit him. She raced towards the sea.

The sand slowed her progress, making every step a labour. She was still fifty metres from the water. Already, her friends had accounted for two of the spiders. Their bodies bobbed in the shallows, fragments of leg and carapace floating in the sea. The remaining four spiders danced through the waves, mincing their legs high and snapping their jaws in a bid to eject Sanjay and Rom from the Web.

Rom slipped, falling beneath the waves, and a triumphant spider advanced upon him and dived, biting Rom on the arm. Rom screamed in pain and fear, the sound filling Ana with terror. As she watched, Rom disappeared in a vortex swirl of multicoloured dots. She imagined him coming to his senses on a Web-couch in America, a world away from the battle.

Now, four spiders inched towards Sanjay, circling him and moving in for the kill. Ana waded into the turgid, green waters of the shallows. She reached out and grabbed the first spider, sickened by its hairy weight as she swung the creature from the water and up the beach, where it landed in a tangle of broken limbs.

She moved to the next spider, but the other two creatures had Sanjay backed up against the side of the boat. He lashed out with his oar, keeping them at bay, but it would be only a matter of seconds before one darted beneath his attack and struck the final bite.

'The house is on Himachal Boulevard, off Patel Marg!' she yelled at him. 'You can't miss it, Sanjay! It's exactly like the house here on the island!'

He looked up at her, but she was unable to tell whether he had heard her. 'Sanjay! Did you hear me? I said the house is on Himachal Boulevard!'

And at that very second a spider darted towards Sanjay, reached out with its snapping jaws and bit him on the upper leg. The frog's mouth opened in a short scream, and then he vanished in a fizz of pixels.

Instantly, the remaining spiders stepped from the water

and walked up the beach, leaving behind the shattered legs and bodies of their companions.

Ana dragged herself from the water, the undertow pulling at her legs, and staggered up the beach.

'I don't know if he heard me!' she cried to herself. 'I just don't know.'

She fell silent as she heard cries and shouts of help from high above. Among the children's voices, she heard Ajay calling her name.

Gripped by panic, Ana hurried up the path to the house on the summit of the island.

CHAPTER NINE

ESCAPE FROM THE WEB

There was a commotion on the lawn when Ana returned.

The children were gathered at the far end, away from the house, holding on to each other and crying. Ana squirmed through the gap in the fence and hurried towards the wailing children. She found Ajay beside Bindra.

'What's wrong? What's happening?'

Bindra looked at her, his face made ugly with anguish. 'Just five minutes ago – *he* came!' Bindra pointed towards the house.

Ana followed the direction of his gesture, but saw no one.

'Who came, Bindra?' she asked.

'Him,' Bindra wailed. 'Look!'

Now Ana could see, standing beside the house and looking out across the ocean, a familiar overweight figure.

'Deepak Rao!' she said to herself.

But why was he here? He had tortured the children enough in real life, why follow them into the Web?

Ana left Ajay with Bindra. 'I'll be back in two minutes, Ajay. I'm going to talk to him.'

'Be careful!' Bindra warned. 'Don't let him harm you!'

'In the real world maybe he can harm me,' Ana said. 'But here he can do nothing. In the Web we are equal.'

She left the children and walked across the lawn. For all

her brave words, as she approached Deepak Rao she felt a flutter of apprehension in her belly.

He was not the young, slim version of Deepak Rao who had appeared in the Web earlier. Now he looked like he did in real life – big-bellied and many-chinned. As Ana came closer, she saw that Rao was in distress. He clutched the wire fence like a man imprisoned, and his cheeks were streaked with tears.

When he saw Ana, he tried to dash the tears from his face with fat fingers. 'What do you want, girl?'

She felt fear block the words in her throat. She told herself that even if he tried to hit her, the blow would not hurt that much. But it was still hard to overcome the fear that she had lived with for so many years.

Ana did not know where the words came from, and looking back on it later she was amazed at what she said. 'Now you know what it's like to be held prisoner. Now you know how unfair it is.'

He tried to bluff her. 'What do you mean?'

Ana stared at him and did not flinch. 'The woman has imprisoned you here,' she said. 'How do you like having *your* freedom taken away, Rao?'

'It's not the same!' he cried. 'I gave you shelter, money to buy yourselves food—'

'You tortured us. You maimed us and blinded us, made us good for nothing but begging for rupees.'

'What kind of life would you have had on the streets had I not taken you in?'

Ana shook her head. 'I don't know,' she answered. 'At worst, I would have begged. I might have found a job. You took away our futures, Rao – you took away any choices we might have had.'

He shook his head. 'You don't understand—' he began.

'I understand that you're evil and greedy. Our afflictions

made your life easy. You couldn't see our suffering, or you chose to ignore it.' She paused there, staring at the fat man before her. 'And for that you've been rewarded.'

He pointed a finger at her. 'I'm in here not because of what I did out there,' he said, 'but because of what I know. The evil witch told me what she was doing here – told me all about her experiments. Then she had me imprisoned so that I couldn't tell the world!'

Ana recalled the first time she had been on the island, when she had seen the woman and Rao walking around this very lawn. Then she had heard Rao ask what the woman was doing here, but they had moved away from where Ana was hidden and she hadn't heard the reply.

Now she felt her pulse quicken. Her throat was dry.

'What?' she asked in barely a whisper. 'What is she doing with the children?'

Rao glanced at her, his lips trembling. 'Do you really want to know?'

'Tell me!'

'You would be better off in ignorance.'

'I said, tell me.'

He laughed in despair, then began weeping. Great tears rolled down his cheeks. He pushed at them with his chubby fingers, for all the world like an overgrown baby.

'She . . . she told me what was happening. I found it hard to believe. I know you think I'm evil, girl – but I never in all my years killed a single soul.'

'What is she doing to us!' Ana demanded.

He took a deep breath. 'She told me that she is experimenting with you – with us. You see, she is very old and very near death, and it is her wish to remain alive for ever.'

'Is that possible?'

'She claims that it is. She can remain alive for ever, not in the flesh and bone body that she possesses now, but in the Web.'

Ana shook her head. 'I don't understand.'

'She plans to live in the Web for ever as a young woman, not the old crone she is now. She will transfer herself into the memory of the Web, but to do that she needs to experiment with others first to perfect the transfer process. That is why you – why *we* – are imprisoned here. We will not be allowed to return to the real world. We will stay here for months and suffer the sickness and nausea that comes of spending too long in the Web. Then we will die, and when our bodies die, the woman will attempt to transfer our identities into the memory of the Web. You've seen the ghosts of some of the children who have died? These are her unsuccessful experiments. They haven't been fully transferred. The woman hopes to transfer herself more successfully into the Web so that she will be able to live here for ever, able to touch and sense and experience everything here just as if it were the real world. Now do you understand why she needs guinea pigs to perfect her transfer technique? We are disposable. We are less than nothing to her. We are the means to an end – the means to her ultimate immortality!'

Ana thought of the ghost of Dilli she had spoken to in the forest. She heard again his pleas for her to help him.

She shook her head in defiance. 'We won't let the woman do this,' she whispered to herself.

Rao gave a great bellow of mirth. 'Fine sentiments, girl! But how can you stop her?'

Ana stared at the fat coward. 'I can stop her and I will!'

'Observe,' said Rao, shaking his arm in the air. 'We have no wristpads to control our stay here. We're imprisoned as if it were a jail made from bricks and mortar.'

'We can escape, Rao,' Ana told him. 'I have friends out in the real world working to do just that.'

He peered at her, suspicious. 'I don't believe you.'

'Do you see me crying?' she asked him. 'Do you see me blubbing like a baby at what the woman hopes to do to us?'

'But how is it possible?' Rao began, a gleam of hope in his eyes.

Ana stared at Deepak Rao. She almost laughed at the pleading tone in his voice. 'I said I could free us from the Web – myself, Ajay and Bindra and all the other children. I said nothing about you, Rao.'

'Would you leave me here to become a wailing ghost?' he cried.

'I think it'd be a just punishment if I left you here while we all escaped,' Ana said. She knew that if Sanjay did what they had planned, then everyone including Rao would be freed from the Web – but Rao did not know that.

'No . . .' he moaned.

'Why *should* I help you, Rao? What have you ever done for me, apart from have my leg removed, and blind my brother?'

'But if you get me out of here, I'll . . . I will—'

'What, Rao?' she asked. 'What will you do to make up for what you did to all of us?'

He shook his head, spreading his hands wide in a pleading gesture. 'Anything,' he babbled. 'Anything at all. Name your price.'

Ana felt excitement rising within her, a sense of power and triumph. 'If we give you your freedom,' she said, 'then out there in the real world, you must give us *our* freedom. We will no longer beg for you, ah-cha? We will beg for ourselves – and you will no longer take in new children and maim them and make them work for you.'

Rao nodded like a pathetically grateful child. 'Of course. Anything, anything.'

'And another thing.'

'Name it.'

'I want your gold.'

He stared down at the gold rings that covered his fingers, the bracelet and watch around his wrist. 'They are yours, all of them. As soon as I am out of here.'

'But how can I trust you, Rao? How do I know you will keep your promise?'

He spread his hands. 'You have only my word of honour,' he said.

She nodded. For what it was worth, his word of honour was all she could hope for.

'Then I'll help you escape,' she said.

She left him beside the fence and returned to the crowd of children at the far end of the lawn.

'What did he say?' Bindra asked.

'Don't worry,' Ana said. 'Deepak Rao will harm no one.'

She took Ajay's hand and drew him to her, kissed the soft skin of his forehead.

She wondered if Sanjay *had* heard her, down there on the beach – if he was now trying to bring about their escape.

If he had not heard her, then surely he would attempt to come here again. It would only be a matter of time before he made it to the house. If, that was, he was able to fight his way past the spiders.

Please, she whispered to herself. Oh, Sanjay, please.

All she could do now was wait.

She sat down with Ajay and stared out at the ocean and the huge sun slipping slowly into the sea. Now and again, great alien whales surfaced, blew a spout of ocean water, and dived.

'We will get out of here soon,' she told her brother.

'Do you mean that, Ana?'

'And when we do get out, I will buy you new eyes, so that you can see again.'

He smiled and laid his head on Ana's shoulder.

It was then, as Ana gazed out at the setting sun and the basking whales, that the world around them began to change.

First, the sun changed colour. From a huge dome of fiery red, it became blue, and then black. The amazing thing was that all around them was still light. The children gasped and pointed. Then the sky changed – became a vast screen like a holo-ad, across which a thousand different images moved. Ana watched, becoming dizzy with the procession of moving scenes. She saw a thousand worlds up there, and a million people walking across the sky like gods.

Around them, the house and the lawn were undergoing a rapid transformation, too. The house winked out of existence, replaced by a house-shaped mosaic of a thousand fractured scenes. Ana could see patches of mountain and river next to scraps of road and city. Faces appeared, staring out at her.

The lawn became a multicoloured quilt, and the island beyond the fence flickered like silver lightning.

The children screamed.

Ajay gripped Ana's hand. 'What's happening?'

Ana stared. 'I think we're leaving the Web,' she said. 'I think Sanjay is saving us . . .'

As she said this, she realized that she could smell something. She inhaled. An irritating, acrid stench filled her nostrils. At first she was unable to identify the smell. It grew stronger, making her eyes water. She choked, coughing.

Then she knew what the terrible stench was.

Smoke!

Suddenly, the world of the Web went mad.

The scene around her flickered on and off. Ana seemed to be existing in two places at once – on the strangely transformed island one second, and the next on the Web-couch in the house.

She heard snatches of screams from the other children.

And then a familiar voice: '. . . get you out of here!'

Screams again – and Ajay crying in fright.

'Quick!' Sanjay's desperate shout. 'Move to the window!'

She was on the Web-couch struggling to free herself.

And then back on the island, trying to make sense of the kaleidoscope of sickening images that swirled around her head.

She saw a face before her, a floating face she recognized. 'Dilli?' she said.

The face whispered. She made out the words, 'Ana, thank you . . .'

The face was fading. 'Ana,' Dilli said, 'you are releasing us from our torment. Thank you . . .' And even as he spoke, his face and his words grew even fainter until they were no more.

The stench of the smoke was making Ana retch.

Another voice sounded close by. 'Ana? Is that you? Quickly!'

She sat up. She was back in the real world. The room was in half-darkness. Figures hurried about her. She tugged off her face mask, pulled the wires from her Web-suit connecting her to the computers. She realized the reason for the half-light was that the room was filled with smoke. Sanjay was rushing from couch to couch, unfastening the children, telling them to get up and move towards the window.

Some children had been in the Web for so long that they could not walk. Others, in the real world, had missing legs, or were blind.

Ana jumped off her couch. She found her crutch where she had left it, picked it up and limped across to help Sanjay.

There were still some children strapped down. The smoke was becoming thick, unbreathable.

She moved awkwardly from couch to couch, unfastening straps, pulling away the face masks and connecting wires, helping the children to their feet. She led them across the room, half-carrying those too weak to hold themselves upright. A knot of children stood beside the open window, identical in the grey Websuits.

She looked for Ajay. She could not tell if he was among the group by the window. She hobbled around the room, peering desperately through the swirling smoke at each couch.

There – Ajay had staggered across the room and was sitting by the door, his face distorted with fear.

'Ajay!' she cried. She limped across to him, choking on the smoke, and dragged him to his feet. He clung to her like a frightened monkey as she half-dragged him across the room.

Sanjay was beside her.

'How did you get in?' she asked.

'I petrol-bombed the lower storey,' he said. 'While they were trying to put it out, I smashed a window and ran through the house. I thought I was never going to find you.' He stared around the room. 'I think that's everyone out of the Web,' he said.

Ana saw a fat shape on a couch across the room. 'No – there's one more!' She started across the room.

Sanjay gripped her arm, halting her. 'I know,' he said. 'It's Deepak Rao. Leave him!'

Before he could stop her, Ana pushed herself across the room and fumbled with the straps binding Rao to the couch. She pulled the mask from his face.

Rao struggled upright, moaning in terror.

For a second, their eyes met. Ana stared at him. Rao

reached out, tears in his eyes, and touched her cheek with his fat fingers.

Ana hurried back to the window.

Sanjay had tied two ropes to the leg of a solid table beside the window. Now he was helping the children over the window ledge and down the rope.

The blind children moved by touch, swarming over the window ledge with a speed that amazed Ana. Those without arms moved just as fast. Two children had legs missing. Sanjay carried one on his back, and Ana lifted the other. The boy's arms fastened around her neck, almost choking her.

Ajay found the rope, followed Sanjay's shouted instructions, and disappeared over the edge.

Behind them, the door exploded inwards and a great plume of flame roared into the room. Ana felt the heat scorch the back of her leg. The children still waiting by the window screamed in terror. Ana looked around her. Parveen sat curled on the floor, sobbing.

Deepak Rao was about to climb over the window ledge. He paused and looked across at Parveen, indecision on his face.

'You must take her!' Ana screamed.

'There's no time,' Rao called back. 'We have to get out!'

'I saved you!' Ana reasoned. 'Now you must save her!'

Rao looked from Ana to Parveen and made his decision. He reached out, whisked Parveen up and placed her on his back. He gripped the rope and lowered himself from the window, face contorted in pain and concentration.

Ana looked around the room. She and the boy she carried were the last to leave. She peered out of the window as Sanjay followed Rao over the ledge. It seemed a long way down to the lawn, and she felt a moment of terrible fear. Then the fire roared like a crazed animal behind her. She threw her crutch out first, watched Sanjay lower himself down the side of the house, then gripped the rope and climbed from the window.

The bricks of the house were hot against her bare foot, and the rope burned her fingers. The boy on her back clung tight, almost strangling her. His weight dragged her down and she feared that at any moment she would be unable to hold on any longer and they would drop.

Above her, tongues of flame came licking from the window. The house was collapsing. The roof fell in with a deafening crash and bricks tumbled all around her.

With a hopeless cry she lost her grip on the rope and fell.

A second later she landed on the lawn and was aware of hands helping her and the boy to their feet. Ana found her crutch, hobbled with the others across the lawn and away from the burning house. She turned and stared at the inferno raging in the darkness.

In twos and threes the children slipped from the grounds of the house, towards freedom. Ana saw Deepak Rao standing in the middle of the lawn staring at the blazing house. She limped towards him and halted. He glanced at her.

'I helped you escape,' she said in a small voice. Now, in the real world, her fear of him had returned. This was the man who had made the lives of many children a misery. Did she really expect him to honour his promise?

His eyes regarded her as if she were an insect, and then something in his expression softened. His hands were a blur of motion. He pulled half a dozen rings from his fat fingers, slipped a gold bracelet from his wrist.

He held out a fist full of gold jewellery that winked and glimmered in the light of the flames, his expression unreadable. Ana reached out and took the gold in her hands. Deepak Rao turned and ran, disappearing rapidly into the darkness.

Sanjay hurried over to her, Ajay at his side. 'Look!' he called, pointing.

A white Mercedes roared up the driveway. As Ana watched, figures hurried from the house towards the car. She recognized the white-coated medics and the tall strong man.

Rajiv, the strong man, was carrying something in his arms – something incredibly old and light. As Ana stared, she made out the bent, frail shape of the woman, with her ancient face and clawed hands.

Their eyes met across the lawn, and for a second Ana felt the woman's rage and hatred directed at her.

The moment passed. The medics and Rajiv dived into the Mercedes. It sped off, turned into the street and roared away into the night.

'She survived,' Ana said to herself. She told Sanjay, then, what the old woman had been doing to the children.

Sanjay took her hand. 'She's old,' he said. 'Time is against her. Maybe . . . maybe this was her last chance, and we put an end to her dreams?'

Ana stared at her new friend, and shook her head. 'I don't think so, Sanjay,' she whispered to herself.

As fire sirens sounded through the night, Ana, Ajay and Sanjay moved from the remains of the house, heading north towards New Delhi.

CHAPTER TEN

ANA AND AJAY

Ana and Ajay sat on the pavement outside the Union Coffee House.

Storm clouds were gathering in the early evening sky, and here and there above New Delhi the holo-ads were flashing on. Ajay slept beside Ana, his head resting on her shoulder.

A car drew up in the street outside the restaurant. Ana carefully moved Ajay's head, found her crutch and stood. As the car door hinged up she pushed herself across the pavement. A rich family climbed out, mother, father and two children, a boy and a girl around her age. The kids hurried past her without a second glance.

Ana thought of the world of the Web, where for a brief time she had been equal.

'Baksheesh,' she called out, pushing herself in front of the man. 'Please spare me ten rupees so that I can eat tonight.'

'Ten rupees!' the woman exclaimed. 'The cheek of the girl!'

'How many rupees will you spend on your meal?' Ana asked. 'One hundred? Two? With ten rupees I can feed my brother and myself for days.'

Embarrassed, the man was sorting through his wallet. 'Here! Now go. Bother us no more.'

Ana accepted the ten rupee note with a triumphant smile.

She returned to the sleeping Ajay, sat down and tucked

the note along with all the others into the purse around her neck.

Earlier that day she had taken Deepak Rao's gold rings and bracelets to a jewel trader in Old Delhi.

'Are these stolen?' the trader had asked after examining the treasures.

'What does it matter to you?', Ana said. 'You'll sell them at a profit whether they're stolen or not.'

The trader glared at the bright little beggar girl, too cocky by half, and bent to inspect the rings once more through his eye-piece.

'I will give you one thousand rupees,' he said at last. 'No more.'

Ana laughed. 'One thousand? Now it's you who's trying to steal them! I'll take four thousand and not a rupee less.'

'Four thousand? Do I look like I was born yesterday, girl?'

And so began half an hour of haggling.

At last, the trader made his final offer. 'Two thousand five hundred rupees. Take it, or leave my premises for ever!'

Ana had taken it, stashed the wad of notes in her purse and hurried back to Ajay.

A taxi pulled up outside the restaurant. Again Ana pushed herself upright and limped across the pavement.

The taxi door opened and a young boy jumped out.

'Sanjay!' Ana said.

'Ana. You said you'd visit me.'

Ana shrugged, smiling shyly. It was a week since Sanjay had rescued her and Ajay and the other children from the Web. That night they had returned to his bungalow, ate and slept in luxury. In the morning, Ana had promised that she would be back soon. But—

She shrugged again. 'I've been busy, Sanjay.'

'Never mind. Look, I've brought you something.' He

reached into the pocket of his jacket and pulled out a small square card. Ana took it – a VR-bar card.

'So you can join us in the Web, Ana. Rom wants to meet you again. I want to introduce you to all my other friends.'

Ana thought of her time in the Web, in Tropicana Bay when she had not been a twelve-year-old beggar girl, but sixteen with two good legs and a beautiful red dress.

Where, for a time, she had been equal.

The thought of experiencing that world again filled her with excitement.

'You will join me, won't you?' Sanjay asked.

'Of course. In maybe two weeks, ah-cha? You see, I want to buy eyes for Ajay.'

They sat on the kerb and talked as the sky darkened.

Later, when the taxi carried Sanjay home, Ana returned to Ajay and rested his head on her shoulder.

That afternoon she had taken Ajay to an eye surgeon in New Delhi. She had paid twenty rupees for the consultation, and waited with apprehension while the surgeon examined Ajay's blind eyes.

At last the grey-haired man had nodded. 'It can be done,' he said. 'But it will be expensive.' His gaze took in Ana's dirty clothing, her one leg and crutch.

'It will cost three thousand rupees,' he told her.

'I'll give you two thousand five hundred,' Ana said, defiant.

The surgeon smiled. 'You are not in any common bazaar here, little girl. My prices are fixed. I charge three thousand rupees to replace damaged eyes.'

Ana tried to work out how long it might take her to earn the extra five hundred rupees. Months, maybe even years. She felt a crushing sense of disappointment. She had hoped that, maybe, in a day or two Ajay would be able to see again.

The surgeon took off his glasses, massaged his eyes. 'Listen to me, girl,' he said. 'In your case, just this once, I'll make an exception. Come back when you have two thousand and six hundred rupees, and I'll give your brother new eyes, ah-cha?'

She had almost danced from the surgery in joy.

She needed just one hundred more rupees. If she begged hard, night and day, she would be able to earn that much in no time at all, perhaps a week or two.

She put an arm around Ajay's shoulders and held him to her. Of course, she could have asked Sanjay for the money. But Sanjay was a friend, and she did not beg money from friends.

And she could always sell the Webcard he had given her. It would be worth well over a hundred rupees. But she would not do that, either. She wanted to save the card. She wanted to meet Sanjay and his friends in the Web in two weeks' time.

She would take Ajay with her – an Ajay who would be able to see the wonderful world of the Web with his own eyes.

Smiling, Ana lay her cheek on Ajay's head and tried to sleep.

Overhead, the monsoon rains began to fall.

WEBSPEAK – A GLOSSARY

AI	Artificial intelligence. Computer programs that appear to show intelligent behaviour when you interact with them.
avatar or realoe	Personas in the Web that are representations of real people.
basement-level	Of the lowest level possible. Often used as an insult, as in 'You've got a basement-level grasp of the situation.'
bat	The moment of transition into the Web or between sites. You can 'do a bat' or 'go bat'. Its slang use has extended to the everyday world. 'bat' is used instead of 'come in', 'take a bat' is a dismissal. (From *Blue And Tone*.)
bite	To play a trick, or to get something over on someone.
bootstrap	Verb, to improve your situation by your own efforts.
bot	Programs with AI.
chasing the fade	Analysing what has happened in the Web after you have left it.
cocoon	A secret refuge. Also your bed or own room.

cog

Incredibly boring or dull. Initially specific to the UK and America this slang is now in use worldwide. (From *Common Or Garden* spider.)

curl up

'Go away, I don't like you!' (From *curl up and die*.)

cyberat

A Web construct, a descendant of computer viruses, that infests the Web programs.

cybercafe

A place where you can get drinks and snacks as well as renting time in the Web.

cyberspace

The visual representation of the communication system which links computers.

d-box

A data-box; an area of information which appears when people are in Virtual Reality (VR).

download

To enter the Web without leaving a Realworld copy.

down the plug

A disaster, as in 'We were down the plug'.

egg

A younger sibling or annoying hanger-on. Even in the first sense this is always meant nastily.

eight

Good (a spider has eight legs).

flame

An insult or nasty remark.

fly

A choice morsel of information, a clue, a hint.

funnel

An unexpected problem or obstacle.

gag

Someone, or something, you don't like very much, who you consider to be stupid. (From *Glove And Glasses*.)

glove and glasses

Cheap but outdated system for experiencing Virtual Reality. The

	glasses allow you to see VR, the gloves allow you to pick things up.
Id	Interactive display nodule.
mage	A magician.
mip	Measure of computer power
nick or alias	A nickname. For example, 'Metaphor' is the nickname of Sarah.
one-mip	Of limited worth or intelligence, as in 'a one-mip mind'.
phace	A person you meet in the Web who is not real; someone created by the software of a particular site or game.
phreak	Someone who is fanatical about virtual reality experiences in the Web.
protocol	The language one computer uses to talk to another.
raid	Any unscheduled intrusion into the Web; anything that forces someone to leave; a program crash.
realoe	See *avatar*.
Realworld	What it says; the world outside the Web. Sometimes used in a derogatory way.
scuttle	Leave the Web and return to Realworld.
silky	Smarmy, over enthusiastic, untrustworthy.
six	Bad (an insect has six legs).
slows, the	The feeling that time has slowed down after experiencing the faster time of the Web.
spider	A web construct. Appearing in varying sizes and guises, these are used to pass on warnings or information

in the Web. The word is also
commonly applied to teachers or
parents.

spidered-off   Warned away by a spider.

spin in   To enter the Web or a Website.

spin out   To leave the Web or a Website.

SFX   Special effects.

strand   A gap between rows of site sky-
                   scrapers in Webtown. Used to de-
                   scribe any street or road or journey.

suck   To eat or drink.

supertime   Parts of the Web that run even faster
                   than normal.

TFO   Tennessee Fried Ostrich.

venomous   Adjective; excellent; could be used
                   in reference to piece of equipment
                   (usually a Websuit) or piece of pro-
                   gramming.

vets   Veterans of any game or site. Ultra-
                   vets are the *crème de la crème* of these.

VR   Virtual Reality. The illusion of a
                   three-dimensional reality created by
                   computer software.

warlock   A sorcerer; magician.

Web   The worldwide network of com-
                   munication links, entertainment,
                   educational and administrative sites
                   that exists in cyberspace and is rep-
                   resented in Virtual Reality.

Web heads   People who are fanatical about
                   surfing the Web. (See also *phreaks*.)

Web round   Verb; to contact other Web users via
                   the Web.

Websuit   The all over body suit lined with
                   receptors which when worn by Web

	users allows them to experience the full physical illusion of virtual reality.
Webware	Computer software used to create and/or maintain the Web.
widow	Adjective; excellent; the term comes from the Black Widow, a particularly poisonous spider.
wipeout	To be comprehensively beaten in a Web game or to come out worse in any Web situation.

OTHER TITLES IN
THE WEB SERIES

GULLIVERZONE by Steve Baxter

February 7, 2027, World Peace Day. It's a day of celebration everywhere. Even access to the Web is free today. It's the chance Sarah's been waiting for, a chance to sample the most wicked sites, to visit mind-blowing virtual worlds. She chooses GulliverZone and the chance to be a giant amongst the tiny people of Lilliput.

But the peace that is being celebrated in Realworld does not extend into cyberspace. There is a battle for survival being fought in Lilliput and what Sarah discovers there in one day will be enough to change her life for ever – providing she can get out to live it . . .

GULLIVERZONE, the fear is anything but virtual.

GULLIVERZONE ready for access.

FEEL UP TO ANOTHER?

DREAMCASTLE by Stephen Bowkett

Dreamcastle is the premier fantasy role-playing site on the Web, and Surfer is one of the premier players. He's one of the few to fight his way past the 500th level, one of the few to take on the Stormdragon and win. But it isn't enough, Surfer has his eyes on the ultimate prize. He wants to be the best, to discover the dark secret at the core of Dreamcastle. And he's found the girl to take him there. She's called Xenia and she's special, frighteningly special.

He's so obsessed that he's blind to Rom's advice, to Kilroy's friendship and to the real danger that lies at the core of the Dreamcastle. A danger that could swallow him whole . . . for real.

DREAMCASTLE, it's no fantasy.

DREAMCASTLE ready for access.

TAKE ANOTHER WALK ON THE WILD SIDE

SPIDERBITE by Graham Joyce

In 2027 a lot of schooltime is Webtime. Imagine entering Virtual Reality and creeping through the Labyrinth with the roars of the Minotaur echoing in your ears? Nowhere near as dull as the classroom. The sites are open to all, nothing is out of bounds. So why has Conrad been warned off the Labyrinth site? There shouldn't be any secret in Edutainment.

Who is behind the savage spiders that swarm around Conrad whenever he tries to enter the site? And why do none of his friends see them? There is a dark lesson being taught at the centre of the Labyrinth . . .

SPIDERBITE, school was never meant to be this scary . . .

SPIDERBITE ready for access.

ARE YOU READY TO GO AGAIN?

LIGHTSTORM by Peter F. Hamilton

Ghostly lights out on the marsh have been the subject of tales and rumours for as long as anyone can remember but the reality is far more frightening than any ghost story.

Something is going wrong at the nearby energy company and they are trying to keep it a secret. Somebody needs to be told. But Aynsley needs help to do it. The Web keeps him in touch with a network of friends across the world and it might just offer him a way in past the company security to find out exactly what's going on.

But the Web works both ways. If Aynsley can get to the company then the company can get to him. And the company has a way of dealing with intruders.

LIGHTSTORM, sometimes it's best to be in the dark.

LIGHTSTORM ready for access shortly.

IS THIS THE END?

SORCERESS by Maggie Furey

A fierce and menacing intelligence is corrupting the very heart of the Web. Vital research data is being stolen. Someone or something is taking control of a spectacular new gamezone. The Web is no longer safe. The Sorceress continues to outwit all who attempt to destroy her, but her time is running out and she will stop at nothing to get what she wants. Someone must stop her.

Only one person has the power to overcome the awesome creator of the Web.

But who could survive a battle with the Sorceress?

SORCERESS ready for access shortly.